Total

Rebecca Miller is a writer and director. She is the author of *The Private Lives of Pippa Lee*, a *Sunday Times* bestseller and Richard & Judy Book Club pick, which she also adapted for screen; *Personal Velocity*, her feature film of which won the Grand Jury Prize at Sundance; and *Jacob's Folly*. Her film work includes *Angela*, *The Ballad of Jack and Rose* and *Maggie's Plan*. Her work has been published in thirty-two languages.

ALSO BY REBECCA MILLER

NOVELS
Jacob's Folly
The Private Lives of Pippa Lee

STORIES
Personal Velocity

FILMS
Angela
Personal Velocity
The Ballad of Jack and Rose
The Private Lives of Pippa Lee
Maggie's Plan
Arthur Miller: Writer

Total

Rebecca Miller

CANONGATE

This paperback edition published in Great Britain in 2023
by Canongate Books

First published in Great Britain in 2022 by Canongate Books Ltd,
14 High Street, Edinburgh EH1 1TE

First published in the USA by Farrar, Straus and Giroux,
120 Broadway, New York 10271

canongate.co.uk

1

British Library Cataloguing-in-Publication Data
A catalogue record for this book is available on
request from the British Library

ISBN 978 1 83885 769 1

Designed by Abby Kagan

Printed and bound in Great Britain by Clays Ltd, Elcograf S.p.A.

For D.

And in memory of Titti

CONTENTS

MRS. COVET   1

I WANT YOU TO KNOW   21

VAPORS   51

TOTAL   69

SHE CAME TO ME   117

RECEIPTS   133

THE CHEKHOVIANS   147

ACKNOWLEDGMENTS   177

MRS. COVET

I
t started with the ladybugs.

The first one was a promise of luck on a spring day as I folded towels in the kids' bathroom. The shiny little bubble moved clumsily up the mirror, seemed actually to waddle in her red armor with its cheerful yellow spots.

> *Ladybug, Ladybug, fly away home,*
> *Your children are crying,*
> *Your house is on fire.*

What's lucky about that?

I leaned over and put my finger up to her; she crawled up on it. I wondered, Are you supposed to make a wish?

Tyler walked in then, eyes puffy from his nap, and pulled down his pants for a pee, utterly unaware of my presence. I watched him, the ladybug balanced on my fingertip, as the manly stream of yellow piss thundered down into the bowl. He pulled up his pants and turned toward the door.

"What about your hands?" I said.

He looked up, only mildly surprised to see me there, then held out his chubby hands for me to wash. I am as ubiquitous as air in this house for my children; often they take as much notice of me as if I were a breeze filtering through the screen door. This doesn't sound too good, I know, but I take pride in it. My kids trust me. They know I'll be there.

Tyler went back into his room. I heard him starting to build an airport. His older brother, Kyle, was still in school. It was two-thirty, and I figured I had time for a quick orgasm before school let out. So I went into our bedroom, slipped under the covers of the unmade bed, and took off my pants.

La petite mort. That's what the French call it. A little death. It is like dying, isn't it? The open mouth, the closed eyes, and how you go out of time for a few seconds—you're nowhere. It's impossible to feel fear while you're coming. I wouldn't care if there were a shark charging at me through the surf.

When I first flirted with Craig in college, we were flipping through an anthology of French poems when we read it there and giggled. *Une petite mort.* Later, when we were in bed together, we whispered it into each other's ears—*une petite mort.* (We were French majors.)

Actual physical sex seems so clumsy and awkward to me these days. My own nudity seems rubbery, numb, this pregnant belly and these thin weak limbs, this rough shock of pubic hair. Sex works much more smoothly in my mind. I never think of anyone but my husband, of course—that would be a real betrayal. I haven't ever been unfaithful to Craig, and I wouldn't. I always turn him into a stranger, though, when I do it: some guy I meet in a bar, or a library. He looks over at me and he just can't help being excited by my huge butt (which I actually do not have).

So I do kind of secretly understand those gay men who say

they just love to make it with strangers. I mean, I would never have the courage personally to go pick up someone I hadn't even been introduced to, and I probably wouldn't even *like* it, if it were real. Or maybe I would. But you know how some people are so disgusted with the idea of certain gay men and how they used to have sex with strangers before AIDS; who knows, maybe they still do, but not all of them do. In fact, the most solid couple I know, aside from me and Craig, are both men—Larry and Dennis, we had them over to dinner last week. They wouldn't dream of picking up a stranger. I am totally non-homophobic—except of course when it comes to my sons, where it does make me mildly nervous, the idea of them being gay, but they're not, I don't think. It's probably too early to tell, though you'd think I have an intuition.

Anyway, the point is, I think there is something sort of heartbreaking about sex with strangers. But at the same time I believe absolutely in fidelity. Because I just can't stand hurting people and I can't stand being hurt. I never wanted a dog—even as a kid—because dogs die after ten or thirteen years, at the most, and then you have to live through that loss again and again *with every dog*. They make you love them, they practically become a person to you, and then they die. Or they get so sick you actually have to have them killed. We had a dog when I was a little girl, a collie, her name was Folly, Folly the Collie, and one day when she was old she got frozen to the ice outside. She couldn't get up anymore. It didn't help warming her up; her legs had gone. She looked up at us helplessly and my dad and I took her to the vet and I held her while they gave her the injection and she peeked up at me with a worried, obedient expression. She knew that I was going to kill her, and she didn't understand why. And then I was supposed to leave the room—or maybe I was scared to stay. I left Folly alone to die. So that was pretty terrible. And I have resisted getting my own boys pets for this reason. The price for love, we all know, is eventually loss, and it's a stiff price, let me tell you. Romantic movies and books are waging a perpetual ad campaign trying to get us all to love with unbridled passion. "Love!" they say. "Love! Love more! Abandon all precaution! Stop being so defensive! Feeling a chill in your marriage? Get a divorce! Marry the repairman!"

I haven't noticed any of the authors of these propaganda pieces putting their home phone numbers inside their book jackets or on the end credits of their films, so that we can call them when we have to go to the hospital and watch the people we have loved with such abandon *die*. They offer no help as we witness our husbands, wives, parents, children, turn blue and green and crumple up like an old balloon; I haven't noticed them offering to put away the garments of the dead, or those who have abandoned us for others. Where are these artists when we need them? Do they offer us any condolence whatsoever? No, because they don't care about us. They don't even think about us. They feed off our yearning to be loved as totally as when we were at our mother's tit, they grow rich off our pathetic need to be happy as embryos, bathed in the warm bath of our mother's blood.

About a week after I saw the first ladybug, I noticed there were five of them in the boys' bathroom. Two in the sink, one in the bathtub, two crawling around on the mirror. Days after that, I was reading Tyler a story in his bed when one of them dropped onto my cheek. It panicked me, I shrieked. I never knew they could fly. They land clumsily, stupidly, and when it's time to take off, they push a little secret pair of wings out from under their shells. Within a month I had counted thirty-five ladybugs in the boys' bathroom alone. Then I started finding them in the bedrooms, our bathroom, the closets. They were flying more and more, and one day one of them was zooming around in crazy circles, and it bit me in the back of the leg. It was an invasion. I started to think they were evil.

But you can't kill a ladybug. It's terrible luck to kill a ladybug.

I started spending more and more time out of the house. Once I dropped the boys at school, I stayed out, got a cup of decaf, went food shopping, even went to a matinee a couple of times. Then I would pick up Tyler from nursery school and we'd go out to an early lunch. The house was becoming a mess. Orange peels under the beds, grime in the toilet bowl. Craig tried to be nice about it. He knows how I get when I'm pregnant. It's hard to describe what happens—it's as though all the walls in my mind slide down like car windows, and the thoughts just float freely around my brain. I find socks in the freezer, notebooks in the linen closet. I once showed up two days late to the dentist. At least I got the time right. But the ladybugs were threatening to be a real problem. I couldn't sleep, I didn't want to be in the house, and I wouldn't let Craig get an exterminator. One night, we were sitting at the kitchen table after dinner. Craig watched as one of the creatures crawled along the edge of a bowl filled with coagulating breakfast cereal. Then he said, "If you need help with the house, I'll get you someone. I'll ask my mother." I burst into tears. I'm not sure if it was relief or a premonition.

The very next day, at 9:00 a.m., my mother-in-law, Carroll Rice, drove up in her new Chevy Impala. She was dressed in baby blue: ironed slacks, matching blue sweater with shoulder pads in it. Her white-blond hair had even taken on a bluish cast. Still in Craig's pajamas, I watched her through the window, my belly pressing against the glass, as she got out of the car, primly brushing imaginary crumbs from her bust, and walked around to the other side. The passenger door opened with ominous slowness; I saw one hand grip the side of the doorframe. A dark head appeared, then swung out of view. A moment passed. Suddenly, an enormous woman heaved herself out of the low car and unfolded herself with difficulty. She must have been six feet tall. Short, dark hair, athletic build. Breasts the size of watermelons. Carroll came up to her shoulder. The two of them strode up to the house. Carroll opened the door with a perfunctory knock, calling out "Daphne!" in her high, singsong voice.

"Hi, Carroll," I said. My underarms were sweating, my teeth were unbrushed, my hair was snarled. Carroll looked me up and down and sighed. She'd had six kids and I doubt she'd let herself look like this for one single morning.

"Honey, this is Nat. She is going to get your life in order."

The Enormous Woman towered over me. Her eyes were a light piercing green; her massive chin seemed clamped onto the rest of her face by a fierce underbite. She was wearing a vast sweatsuit the color of concrete. "I hear you need a little help with the house," she said.

"Well," I said. "I—I . . . think I do. We just thought we'd try . . ."

"You sit tight, honey," Nat said. "You don't look too good. I'm a trained nurse, so calm down." I sat.

Carroll looked at me smugly. "I am so glad you finally let me help you," she whispered.

Nat made us both tea, then set about cleaning the kitchen, whistling loudly, with vibrato. After a while, she thundered upstairs and turned the radio on. I never even showed her around the house. She figured it all out for herself.

Later, drying myself off from my shower, I could hear the sermon she was listening to on the radio. A man's voice was saying, "But the question is not what you need. The question is: *What does Jesus need?* And the answer is easy—because the answer is always the same: *Jesus needs your love.*" By the time I emerged from my room, Nat had found a place for everything in the house. Anything that could fit inside another thing got crammed in there. It didn't matter if it made no sense. She put hair elastics inside egg cups. Magic Markers in the salad bowl. The place looked immaculate, but a lot of things went missing.

After a day or two, I began to suspect that Nat was killing the ladybugs. There were fewer and fewer of them around. Once I found twenty dead bodies on a windowsill. I sniffed, but I couldn't smell chemicals. Why were they dying? "It's the end of their season," said Nat. But still I suspected her. So many ladybugs ought to have brought something hugely lucky to our lives. Killing them could bring calamity. I started to fret, and whenever I hadn't felt the baby move for more than an hour, I poked it till it squirmed.

Nat cooked, too. The fare was plain and fairly tasteless,

but the kids loved it: lasagna, spaghetti with meatballs, fried fish, baked beans. After she was done with the cleaning on that first day, at around one, I expected her to leave, but all she did was put on an apron and start chopping. When the kids were home, she had them doing chores. Tyler walked around with a cleaning rag hanging from his belt, a sponge in one hand. Both boys loved working for Nat. She combed their tousled hair, tamed the curls I loved and slicked them back with water. She started talking about buzz cuts. With the house cleaned, the kids occupied, and dinner in the oven, all I had to do was read and wait for Craig to come home. I spent more and more time in my room. Nat fussed over me. In bed for ten minutes, I'd hear a knock on the door, see her giant silhouette framed by the doorway. "You hungry?" I ate three meals a day, plus egg sandwiches at eleven, a bowl of beans at four, I gained fifteen pounds in a month. My doctor was astounded and relieved that I was up to a normal weight. I didn't tell him that I barely ever walked, ate all day, rarely saw my children. Nat was turning me into an invalid. And I was beginning to realize that Carroll thought I'd been one all along. Hiding in the hall one night, I heard her talking to Craig in her rough whisper. "I tell you, Nat has saved you. Saved you all."

"It wasn't that bad, Ma," said Craig in a cracked voice—always conciliatory, always making less of things, always talking women down.

"*Wasn't that bad?* You're like one of those frogs. If you put a frog in cold water and heat it slowly it won't notice, and before you know it—"

"You have a boiled frog. I get it."

"Admit the house is running better."

"Absolutely. And I thank you."

"She needed this, Craig."

"I know."

"She's fragile."

"She's been under stress, she's fine."

They moved away at that point and I couldn't hear, but two days later, Craig started talking about therapy. God, forgive the mother of my husband.

One afternoon, with nothing else to do, I took off my dress and looked into the mirror. My hips and thighs had puffed up, thanks to Nat's forced feedings, my belly stuck out, but my arms and legs were still skinny. I looked like someone had started to blow me up but stopped before the limbs were fully inflated. There was a dark line drawn down the center of my torso, as if by a Chinese brush. It traveled from between my breasts all the way to my pubis, bifurcating my belly, as if marking me for some operation. How strange pregnancy is. I still can't get over it. To house a baby inside. It makes me feel anonymous, animal. That day, as I stood in front of the mirror, I felt the most intense need to meet this baby. I suddenly had to see its face. This image of me I saw covering up my child—I wanted to claw it away like clay. I needed to break the spell of containment, confinement; I needed to escape from Nat. I wanted to scream. And then—I swear to God it happened this way, I am not making this up—my water broke. As I was standing there naked in front of the mirror, warm liquid traveled down my legs and gathered in a pool at my feet. Two months early. I put on some sweats and called the doctor. Left the kids with Nat. Thank God she was there,

I thought, as I rushed out the door with Craig. My dear husband's face looked pinched; he avoided my gaze. He was frightened. Seven months can be enough, but not always. I knew what he was thinking. He was thinking, If we lose this baby, she won't survive.

They cut me open and lifted him out of me. After, I looked down at the ruby-red gash in my abdomen, glistening like a fleshy flower, my legs warm, numbed, itchy from anesthesia. The doctor held the baby up. He was silent. Moving faintly. Blue. He was handed away. Two masked nurses massaged him wordlessly under orange light. I asked to hold him. No one answered. They kneaded his flesh, trying to coax his reluctant spirit back through the threshold of the world, where it hovered, undecided. Then I heard the wail, fine as a silken thread, floating through the air and I knew he would live. I knew this one was fine, just as I had known my baby sister would die from the moment I held her in my arms, though I did not know it in thoughts. She lasted two months. A child without a destiny. Sixty-one days stamped on her hand. Virginia.

The baby had to stay in the hospital for a while, and so did I. Every night, Craig came to see us and told us how the boys were doing. Nat had shaved their heads. She said there was a head lice scare in school, but I doubted that. She had always wanted them shorn. Then there was church. She had taken them twice in one week. Craig said she even went out and bought them new, Christian-looking clothes. We laughed about it. She was living in the house. Of course she was—how else could Craig get to work by eight?

I felt so peaceful once the baby was born. I felt like I would never plan a thing again. I was cocooned in the present, all alone with baby Adam. He had to be in an incubator the first couple of days, when I wasn't breastfeeding him, but after that they let me keep him in my room. I just stared into his face for hours. The truth is, I was a little wary about going back to real life.

But finally the day came. We drove up to the house, and I saw Kyle, my big-boned boy, walking outside with the garden hose. He had a crew cut and was wearing a red-and-white-checked shirt tucked into his jeans. He looked like something out of *Leave It to Beaver.* "Hey!" I said. He ran to the car and looked at me shyly. He'd only been to the hospital to visit twice. He was getting used to life without me. As he peered through the back window to take a look at the baby, I wondered: If I die, how long will he remember my face, my voice? How long till he never dreams about me anymore? The main thing I loved about being a mother was being indispensable. The front door opened and Nat stood wearing a maroon sweatsuit, her hand on Tyler's shoulder. I got out of the car and hugged both boys.

"I hate the baby," Tyler announced.

"Oh, now," said Nat, "he's your brother. He's gonna be your buddy. For now he's just a baby." She reached in, cooing, and took Adam from the car seat, set him on her mammoth breast, where he looked as small as a ferret. I felt a mixture of envy and relief. I was so tired.

"You go up and nap," said Nat as we walked into the sterilized kitchen. "I'll bring him up when he starts rooting." I climbed the stairs gratefully, the incision in my belly burning. Craig followed me. It was so amazing to be able to walk upstairs with no kids following us. Craig lay close beside me, his light blue irises magnified behind his round glasses. The thing about Craig is, his parents were divorced when he was eight; secretly he lives in fear that one day he'll fall out of love with me and leave, and I'll turn into a bitter and unlovable woman like his mother. So I never know if his love is real or if it's just distilled guilt. But I knew at that moment he just plain loved me.

"Well, you did it again," he said.

"I'm a little scared."

"He's going to be fine. I'm glad Nat is here."

"Me, too. How much are we paying her, anyway?"

He shrugged. "She's a present from my mother."

That night at dinner, as we were tucking into Nat's famous lasagna and chopped salad, the baby sleeping peacefully in his bassinet, a fight erupted between Kyle and Tyler. Kyle was trying to steal a cherry tomato from Tyler's plate. "Thou shalt not covet thy neighbor's tomato," said Craig. I stood up to wash some more. Nat shot up fast instead, chuckling. "My husband calls me Mrs. Covet," she said, washing the tomatoes in a sieve. Craig and I looked up at her, surprised.

"I didn't know you were married, Nat," Craig said. Nat put her hand on her hip in mock outrage.

"What'd ya think, I was an old maid? He calls me Mrs. Covet 'cause whenever he orders something in a restaurant, I change my order so's I can have what he's having, 'cause it always sounds so much better than what I ordered. Mrs. Covet. That's me." From that night, Craig and I started calling Nat "Mrs. Covet" when we were alone.

Now that the baby was born I felt a little clearer in my

head. And my life was so easy with Nat in charge. She had turned out to be the Mercedes of baby nurses. She kept the baby changed, bathed, in clean clothes. She gave him to me when he was about to be hungry. He was the most contented baby I had ever seen. I looked back on the other two and marveled that I had been able to cope at all by myself. Since my sister Virginia died I had been so scared that something would happen to my babies. Now, with Nat here, I felt safe. She was a nurse. She would be able to handle any emergency. I started taking better care of myself—got a manicure and pedicure, had my hair blown out. I looked fat around the middle, but healthy. No one could believe I had just given birth. Craig and I went out to dinner. We fooled around. I started feeling better about myself, and even daydreamed about going to grad school one day.

One morning, I came upstairs and found that Nat had moved the baby's crib into her room. That way, she said, the minute he cried in the night, she could bring him in to me. It would save me getting out of bed. I thought that was a little strange. I said, "It's okay, I don't mind getting up, I like hearing him breathe next to me." She seemed a little put out by this, but she heaved and huffed the crib back into our room.

After a few days had passed, she started saying I should think about weaning him. I had fed both the other boys myself for six months, but Nat thought that was extravagant. "They get everything they need in the first few weeks, after that it's just comfort."

"What's wrong with comfort?" I asked.

"This one you're not going to spoil," she said. I thought that was an outrageous thing to say; we had a fight. She calmed me down by saying she had fallen in love with our family. She thought I was a terrific mother; my kids were the best kids she'd met aside from her own. That was the first I heard of her three children—two girls and a boy, grown now and moved away. Nat was a dark horse.

The next thing that happened was a sign, one I didn't read correctly. I was woken in the middle of the night by the sound of singing. At first I blended it into my dream. Then I opened my eyes. Adam's crib was empty. I got up and went into the hallway. The singing was coming from Nat's room. I opened the door. She was lying in her bed, Adam beside her sucking on her pinky. She blushed and muttered something about wanting to give me a few more minutes of sleep. I was furious. I took the baby back into my room, locked the door, and nursed him. The next morning, Craig thought I had overreacted. "She wanted to give you a little sleep."

"He needs a feed in the night," I said. "I am his mother. I don't mind doing it. It's normal."

"Daphne," he pleaded, in a voice of contained exasperation.

I kept the baby with me all the next day. Nat pretended nothing had happened and she didn't try to take Adam from me. She busied herself with the other kids, cooked dinner, and then she put her coat on. We all looked at her, confused. She explained that she had to look in on her husband and tidy up her house. She would be back Monday. It was Thursday. I knew she was punishing me for what had happened the night before. Mrs. Covet was letting me know that she could live without my children. The question was: Could we live without her? The long weekend was tough, as it turned out, but we made it. It was nice just being the family again. We ordered in pizza, watched a movie, went out to breakfast. We were sloppy. The kids got into our bed on Sunday morning and we had all three of them with us. It felt good. But when Nat appeared on Monday morning, I was glad to see her, happy to hand over the baby so I could bring the boys to school, come home, and take a nap. When I got home, though, Nat's truck was gone. I walked into the house, calling her name. I went into every single room. I went to the basement, where the washing machine was. I went into the yard. My heart was racing; tears stung my eyes. The first thing I thought of was, she had to drive him to the hospital. He stopped breathing. That was what happened with Virginia.

This is how it happened: My mother brought her home in a striped blanket, a tiny woolen hat on her head, eyes shut tight, mouth pursed, fists clenched. I was five. I wanted to hold her all the time. Sometimes my mother let me give her a bottle. I loved the way she looked up at me so earnestly, her lips tugging at the rubber teat, tiny pools of milk gathering at the corners of her mouth. One afternoon, my mother had put the baby down for her nap. I had my friend Tammy over. We were pretending to be witches. We danced down the hall outside my mother's room, muttering incantations, casting spells. We spied the baby's crib and saw her little form huddled there under her striped blanket. I think I started it. I'm not sure, but I think I did. I said, "We're going to take her away! Take her away! Take her away!" We were whispering diabolically, giggling, falling over ourselves, two witches stealing the soul of an infant. Eventually we got bored and went into the kitchen for peanut butter sandwiches and milk.

The next morning, when I woke up, the sky was still dark outside my window. I sat up and felt the cold air, took my sweater from the end of the bed, and pulled it over my head. I tiptoed down the hall to my parents' room and peeked in the door. They were asleep. Virginia was in her crib; I could see her body under the blanket. I couldn't make out her face, though. It felt strange to be up before the baby; it was always her cry that woke me. It felt lonesome. I walked into the kitchen. The linoleum was frigid beneath my bare feet. I thought how proud my mother would be if I made my own breakfast. I tried to pour myself a bowl of cereal, ended up scattering cornflakes all over the table. As I was opening the refrigerator, on my toes, stretching my hand up to reach the milk, I heard my mother screaming. I ran down the hall, but my father blocked the door. "Go to your room," he said. I heard my mother crying out, "I want my baby! I want my baby! I want my baby!" I went into my room and sat on my bed, held my pillow to my chest and prayed. Eventually, the ambulance came.

During the funeral, I stared at my sister's tiny white casket, willing it to open, trying with all my might to force the lid to move even an inch. If I could kill her, perhaps I could make her live, as well. But there was no magic in me that day. I never told anyone what I had done. The guilt settled into me like a leaf falling to the ground, to be covered by other leaves and snow and earth. It melted into my being.

Nat had taken Adam to the hospital. That had to be it. I called Craig. He called the hospital. She hadn't come in. We called Nat's cell phone. It was off. Craig picked up the kids and brought them home. I called the police. Night fell. My mind turned one thought over and over, like a tumble dryer: Mrs. Covet stole my baby.

I was up all night, though I must have drifted off at some point, because I remember dreaming about ladybugs; they were crawling all over me. I woke up thinking about bad luck. On the TV, a documentary was showing: In close-up, an Iraqi woman was tearing her hair. She was screaming, staring into the camera, her face contorted by fury. A blindfolded baby lay in a glass box. I didn't understand. I tuned in late. The British commentator spoke so fast. There was no medicine for her baby? Something terrible had happened to its eyes. Oh, Jesus Christ. In the desert, men in gas masks jumped off a truck. They carried machine guns. They were on their way here. All these years, without knowing, we have reached our arms around the world, dug our thumbs into that baby's eyes. We have made him blind. And now that baby's mother wanted to blind my children. She wanted to slide into their beds while they slept and breathe poison into their little pink mouths. They would wake incoherent, flailing, blind. It was my fault. I remember how smug I felt years ago when I heard the word "sanctions" against Iraq. Such a comforting, peaceful word—like a mother's hand holding back a flailing toddler. Craig turned the TV off. I couldn't look him in the eye. It was his mother who had brought Mrs. Covet into our house. His mother who hated me. Craig knew what I was thinking.

At dawn, the phone rang. They found her in Florida, picked her up in a convenience store buying pretzels. She was carrying the baby. Adam was all right. She didn't want to harm him. She just wanted him, that was all. We got on a plane with the kids and flew to Fort Lauderdale. They had the baby in the hospital there. We stayed in a hotel that night, me and Craig and the three boys. We watched the news. And there on the screen was Mrs. Covet, with a serial number under her massive chin. She looked like a hardened criminal in that picture. "Woman Kidnaps Month-Old Baby." She had no record. That's what the police said. She had been a nurse for twenty years. A married woman with three grown children, and one day she just snapped. Fell in love with our family, like she said. All that time with us, she had yearnings, she was in pain. None of us noticed. We treated her like a joke. We didn't care what was going on inside her, as long as she took care of us. Now she was in prison for kidnapping, all because she loved our baby too much. I felt bad in a way. Too much love had wrecked her life.

It's nearly light. The older children will be up soon. I cling to these moments before the day begins. I hear the baby's breathing changing; he will wake up soon. I feel the tingling pang of milk filling my breasts; a drip of it trickles down my abdomen. My third boy. He is still so new. His soft pink mouth opens, reaches out for my nipple. Eyes still shut, he roots around like a piglet. When he latches on and tastes the milk, his eyelids flutter, his eyes roll back in his head. Desire. Satiation. Desire. That's the story of his day. I am the warmth, the smell, the anchor. He is still nearly blind, innocent to meaning; he is like a pebble, a shell, a rabbit. He is no one, he is ancient, he has a face like a very old man, toothless mouth agape, staring both into and out of the void. I stay with him always.

I WANT YOU TO KNOW

Joad took Andrew's calloused hand as they approached the big river house. They had been invited for ten past seven, just in time for sunset. She imagined how they must look from a distance at that moment: a shaggy giant escorting a child. This physical disparity was an especially popular aspect of their blog: *Joad and Andrew: Living Life from Scratch*, a brightly illustrated farm diary with a growing number of followers, mostly youngish city people toggling between Joad's recipes for soaked breakfast porridge and real estate listings up the Hudson. Joad, with her short black shag and high cheekbones, contrasted beautifully with ruddy Andrew, whose rawboned face, bulbous nose, and one drooping eyelid lent him an aura of early-settler depth—at least in photographs, of which there were many on the site, capturing the couple planting and harvesting, Joad kneading dough, and Andrew fixing machinery. Joad wrote the blog in a voice both cheerful and down to earth, making their way of life seem so appealing that the reader's mouth watered as their envy was aroused by her descriptions of the warmed-up apple pie the couple often ate for breakfast, the pork chops from their neighbor's hog, the soups and the stews and the time spent walking in the woods, gathering mushrooms. It had only been eleven months, but Joad and Andrew's foray into self-determination had begun to make a splash.

Their steps crunched the pebbles of the long drive as the river house drew nearer, an imposing, square mansion painted dove gray with scarlet shutters. They had been told to walk around the side to the porch. As they complied, they saw, like a carved figure at the prow of a great ship, a statuesque woman gazing down at them, the ripples of her long white dress seemingly frozen in place, a bright orange cocktail glowing in her hand.

"At last!" exclaimed Colleen Prentiss in a shredded voice. She opened one powerful arm as if to hug the air, clinking the ice in her drink. Mounting the steps to the colonnaded porch ahead of Andrew, Joad took the woman in: around seventy, she was beautiful, golden, with a broad, beaming face that exuded privilege and goodwill. Colleen shook both their hands and ushered them onto the porch, emanating an aggressive, spicy scent that made Joad's throat constrict. "I've been dying to meet you two for ages, but Trevor has been keeping you to himself!" she declared. Trevor Prentiss, Colleen's son, had sold Joad and Andrew a dilapidated 1920s farmhouse on three acres of land for under market value a year earlier. The stubborn colony of raccoons that resided in the long-empty house accounted for the low price, they assumed. They'd chased off the animals, sealed up the gaps in the walls and floorboards, and scrubbed every surface with bleach—but only a week ago, Joad had glanced out the kitchen window after midnight to see three of the wily creatures, hands up on the sill, peering in at her with what she took to be curiosity and longing.

Joad and Andrew took their front-row seats on the grand porch and gaped at the Hudson River Valley sunset, which spread its legs with lurid abandon, revealing electric-blue mountains etched into the rosy sky, Creamsicle-orange clouds floating like torn cotton puffs, and the river glowing fuchsia, the colors changing and intensifying by the instant. Joad's gaze slipped along the glowing hills, panning left to follow the now-purple current, and landed in a startling close-up of Colleen, two feet away, scrutinizing her greedily.

"What combination of genes could have created that spectacular face?" Colleen wondered aloud.

"Sorry?"

"I'm curious about your ancestry. I've been thinking Eskimo, Gypsy, Mongolian . . ."

"Oh," said Joad. "I'm Chinese Irish Native American."

"Tell me how that happened," said Colleen with an expectant stare.

"Oh, um . . . My . . . great-great-grandfather came from Canton Province to work on the railroads in California and . . . he met my great-great-grandmother, who we think was Chumash. And then . . . it was kind of a big mix from there on in, but mostly Chinese and—and Irish."

"A great face," pronounced Colleen, taking a sip of her

drink. And then, turning to Andrew with a perfunctory smile, she asked, "And you?"

"Scotch Irish."

"I find it fascinating," said Colleen, turning from Andrew back to Joad, "where people originate. I am Huguenot, and Viking—and Welsh, if pressed." Just then, Trevor Prentiss emerged from inside the house. His graying blond hair curled around his head in Roman style, and he wore a benevolent expression, his head cocked, hands clasped against his narrow chest, like a middle-aged elf. "And Trevor's father added Sephardic to that mix," Colleen concluded.

"Talking bloodlines?" asked Trevor, his voice set high up in the belfry of his nose.

"You two tell Trevor what you would like to drink," Colleen said. "Choose anything you like. As he may have told you, Trevor is a restaurateur," she added dryly.

"We're easy," said Andrew. "Whatever you're having."

"Negronis, then," said Colleen, draining her glass and shaking it at her son, who collected it and disappeared inside. Just then, a very large, wet, white dog exploded up the stairs and onto the porch. Hysterically enthusiastic, he bounded in circles, releasing high-pitched shrieks and an arc of cold river water, anointing the guests, then threw his paws up on his mistress in a climax of devotion. "Chet. Chet!" scolded Colleen, attempting to wipe a muddy paw print from her breast. "Oh Christ. Here." She snapped her fingers, and the dog promptly lay on his back. Then Colleen leaned over, grabbed his furry cock, and proceeded to masturbate the animal matter-of-factly as she resumed the conversation, craning her neck to look up at Andrew and Joad, and inquiring, "Where were you living before you came here?" Andrew, frozen, his eyes glued to her face, compulsively listed their history backward: renting a few acres of farmland farther upstate; before that, the collective homestead in Oregon; and, in their early twenties, the blur of life on the road, living paycheck to paycheck with no fixed abode, working boats and ski resorts— whatever they could find. Joad sat mute, trying to recall if she'd ever heard Andrew speak so much to a stranger. Trevor entered with the drinks on a battered silver tray and shook his head at his mother, smiling indulgently as he handed them their cocktails.

"Mom's at it again," said Trevor.

"It's the only thing that calms him down," Colleen explained, her arm jiggling mechanically as the dog's eyes glazed over.

"How is everything going with the house?" asked Trevor.

"We're getting there," said Andrew.

"Trevor bought that place as something to fix up and flip," said Colleen. "Pardon my vulgarity. But when I heard a nice young couple wanted to run an organic farm on the land, I told Trevor to sell it to you as is, for exactly what he paid, damn the profits." The dog flopped over to his side, seemingly unconscious.

"We appreciate that," said Andrew.

"This view," exclaimed Joad. "It's incredible."

"This house was once a boardinghouse. All the painters stayed here, at one time or another."

"The De Vrieses owned it, right?" asked Andrew.

"Yes, they did," said Colleen. "For a century. They started as a grand Dutch family and decade by decade ran that legacy right into the ground."

"I know Buddy De Vries," Andrew offered. "He runs the dump."

Joad imagined Buddy De Vries, a small old man with a twisted mouth who manned the dump on hot days shirtless, deeply tanned, his fuzzy back and shoulders glistening as he tossed bags of trash into the landfill, living in this celestial locale. But there was a time when the Dutch owned everything up here. Colleen offered them another drink; they declined. They were hungry, and had been discussing what they might be offered for dinner all afternoon.

"Well, I hope you'll come again soon," said Colleen.

Walking back down the long driveway, Joad said, "We should get a dog."

"What, aren't I enough for you?"

"That was—oh my God—"

"Do we have anything in the fridge?"

Joad felt Trevor's cocktail loosening her movements as she dropped two hamburger patties onto the hot grill. Swaying her hips from side to side, she listened to the meat spit and sizzle to a background of birdsong. She turned the patties over and walked into the house. In the kitchen, Andrew was making salad and drinking a glass of wine. Joad came in, took the glass he offered, and glanced outside to see a raccoon on its hind legs tossing a hot burger back and forth between its small black hands as it reversed into the woods. She took her phone out to film it, but it was too late. All she got was swaying bushes.

They shared the remaining burger and salad, and then a carton of ice cream.

"Nobody really owns a house," Joad mused as she licked her spoon.

"We sure as hell better own this one," said Andrew.

"I know we technically own it," said Joad, "but . . . I mean . . . the last people who lived here thought they owned it, too."

"They did own it."

"But they only owned it because they paid money for it."

"Pretty standard reason."

"And Trevor thought he owned it. And the raccoons thought they owned it—and actually this land was probably stolen from the Mohicans. At least they knew they didn't own it . . ."

"Are you drunk?"

"Shut up," she said, laughing. "I just mean that land, and places, are actually all just on loan. The grass, the snakes, and everybody, doesn't know, they don't know that, we're, you know, that we own them." She gave up. Her cheeks reddened. Words so often failed her.

Andrew unfolded himself and stood, tall, wide, too big for the low room.

"Why are you doing this?"

"What?

"You know how much this place means to me."

He went upstairs and left her staring at her empty bowl.

By the time she joined him, Andrew was asleep—or pretending to be. He had left her light on and put a glass of water on the floor, by her side. He couldn't help being kind. She switched off the light and lay in the dark, her chest tight. Andrew had sniffed out something in her—the part of her that wasn't sure. Putting the down payment on this house and land with their savings had been the crowning achievement of their lives together, and the dead end of their once-nomadic existence. They were tied to the land now. With her blundering comments about ownership, Joad had cast a shadow on their shared dream of going back to something Edenic, pure, and real—*Joad and Andrew: Living Life from Scratch*—sullied their *brand*, even, she thought viciously—and she felt guilty, but also angry. As she lay there, hot tears pooled in her ears. She promised herself that tomorrow she would be different.

The next morning, she woke before Andrew, humming with energy to attack the house. Up until now they had been half camping. The sunniest corner of the kitchen had been cleared and staged for baking shots—they'd even managed to salvage a slab of marble to make it look upscale—yet just off camera, the bare wood floors were muddy, the cabinets warped and slanted, the table was a metal foldout. There was one lamp in the parlor, which at night gave off a measly smudge of light, and their bedroom was furnished with a mattress on the floor and a couple of apple crates. It was time to transform this into a place where humans lived. And a baby human, possibly, if her calculations were correct.

The hayloft was piled with generations of castoffs. Andrew had told Trevor not to throw anything out after the sale; there might be some useful stuff up there. Joad tied a kerchief over her thick hair, marched to the barn, climbed the rickety ladder to the loft, and stood there, hands on her hips, scanning rusted farm tools, a plastic hobbyhorse, pieces of an ancient loom, a rotting roll of pink insulation, a box of naked Barbies . . . Joad was about to start back down the ladder when she spotted, in the far corner, a small secretary desk peeking above the wave of junk as though trying not to drown. Joad picked her way over to it. Close now, she saw it had numerous drawers and spindly legs. The wood, she knew, was walnut. She rocked it back and forth; the joints were solid. It would need to be stripped and oiled, but it could be lovely. It would fit in the small empty space off the kitchen Joad had earmarked as her extra room, where she planned to update the spreadsheets for the farm, work on recipes, and write the blog. She could keep seeds in the drawers, maybe bills. The delicate desk promised organization, calm, femininity, a break from mud. After lunch, she and Andrew carried it above their heads, trailing spiderwebs, through the detritus. They maneuvered it down the ladder, through the barn, and outside into the heat, scattering a few stray chickens, then set it down on the cracked driveway, where it perched on its slender legs, smeared in dust, silky spider threads floating in the breeze.

Joad opened the drawers and emptied their contents into a cardboard box: a Reagan button, paper clips, faded color photographs of blond children. One small drawer was stuck. Careful to avoid damaging the wood, she left it alone. She wiped down the desk with a damp cloth and let it dry in the sun while she transplanted lettuces with Andrew, gently removing each tiny green plant with its square of soil and roots from the tray, lowering it into a hole in the ground, and patting the dirt flat around it. At three, Andrew stood.

"We better get going," he said.

They'd both recently landed side hustles in a restaurant in the neighboring town. Andrew was hired as a bartender three nights a week, Joad as a server for five. Before service started, they sat on the veranda of the place with the rest of the staff eating pesto pasta, looking out at the few expensive shops on the main drag, none of which they could afford.

"Isn't it weird how some kinds of towns have no pharmacy or barbershop or grocery store, but they do have gourmet ice cream and ceramics?" said Joad.

"That's the gift of artists to a community," said Andrew.

"I like artists. But they do tend to fuck a place up," she said. The cook cracked up at this. Without warning, Trevor Prentiss appeared beside the staff table, his clasped hands lifted to his chest. Joad, confused, looked up at him.

"Trevor! Hi. We're not open yet."

"This is my place!" explained Trevor in his strangled

voice—a masculine voice put through some kind of aggression strainer.

"You're the owner?" said Andrew.

"One of them. Martissa told me she'd hired a couple new people, I can't believe it's you guys!"

"Me neither," said Andrew.

"I'm rarely here, I have another place in Red Hook. Al Fresco?"

"Oh, yeah . . ."

"My wife loves the pesto pasta," he said, smiling down at all the plates. Joad looked up at him sharply. She had not expected a wife. "It's really good," she said vaguely as the rest of the staff watched the interaction.

"Good to see you guys. My mother would love to have you back." Trevor beamed his last and walked back into his restaurant. The hushed group gradually came back to life.

The next day was Saturday; Joad and Andrew brought boxes of vegetables and eggs to the farmers' market in Hudson. By 8:00 a.m. they had set up in the municipal parking lot, and a line formed quickly before their stall. As she weighed produce and made change, Joad kept thinking about the little rescue desk. That afternoon, returning home, she took a "before" picture, then went straight to work, painting stripper over its entire surface. Suddenly exhausted, she lay down on the hot driveway, shut her eyes, and fell asleep. When she woke, the varnish was bubbling up from the wood. With a rubber wedge, she scraped away the gray sludge, wiping each load onto a rag, exposing the grain. As she did so, she noticed a small, flat button inside the upper part of the desk, where the stuck drawer was. She pressed the button; the drawer sprang open. She removed it and looked inside: nothing but a hair tie with fine blond hairs wound around it and a clump of onion-skin typing paper that had been folded, rolled, and pressed flat. On its side, some words were written in tiny letters. She held it close. "I want you to know" had been scrawled in leaky ballpoint. The "o" in "know" had a little comet's tail of smudged ink trailing from it. Joad slipped the wad of paper into her shirt pocket, carried the desk into the garage, cleaned off any residual varnish with turpentine, sanded it, then wiped it down again. And now, her favorite part: she rubbed a bees-wax balm into the naked wood with a fresh, white cloth. The buttery smell of beeswax was comforting and joyous to Joad. It smelled like optimism to her, like clean, honest work, and brought her back instantly to her father's woodshop. As she pressed the cloth in careful rounds, the flame pattern in the desk's center darkened magically, and she thought of the myths about people who rub old oil lamps and djinns come out to do their bidding. Wouldn't it be great to have a djinn come out of this desk, Joad thought. A clean bathroom would be the first thing she would ask for. Next, no more waitressing. When she was done, Joad walked outside where the last of the sun was glimmering through the leaves. She could hear the far-off whine of Andrew's tractor and the pulse of the tree frogs ringing out all around her. She lay down on the still-warm driveway and gazed up at the pink clouds, then piled her shirt under her head as a pillow. She felt something in the front pocket and pulled out the clump of typing paper. "I want you to know," said the tiny letters. Joad straightened out the creased, yellowing pages and began to read.

I found this typewriter by the side of our road last week while I was walking back from town. It's electric and works. I don't know why anyone would throw it away except if they just purchased a personal computer and figured some person who needed an electric typewriter might come by and say, "Hey!" I didn't need a typewriter, but I did say "Hey" when I saw this machine. It's cream-colored, and has a sort of nubbly texture to its hard surface. I lugged it up half a mile of dirt road. I couldn't believe it when I plugged it in, pushed the switch, and it hummed— a strong, manly hum. The sound of it reminds me of JP when we first met. He seemed like nothing could knock him down or even surprise him. He knows how much salt to put into the pasta water and when the noodles are cooked without tasting, without a watch. Whenever I ask him how he knows, he just taps his temple with his forefinger, squinting his eyes and smiling. He does that gesture a lot. He makes another, similar gesture, with *two* flat fingers tapping against his temple while *frowning*. This means that I have done something stupid or nuts.

At the moment, I am sitting here in my nightgown typing, and my elbows are sort of clamped to my sides so my tits will somehow be held up, which is hopeless, but I can't go upstairs and get a bra because JP is on the floor next to the chest of drawers. It isn't even light yet.

I attended the University of Connecticut for two years. There I learned to think for myself. Then, some time after, I forgot. I am not sure how this transformation occurred. In fact I wonder if perhaps I found this typewriter so that I can work it out. So that once and for all I can trace the point of decay (which I can't believe was hereditary. My parents are a little boring, but that's not mental illness. Not yet anyway. Though I'm sure one day the psychiatric community will come up with a drug to combat repetitive storytelling and inane laughter). Here's how I joined the army: I had been to a club and gotten tossed around the mosh pit so much I thought I maybe had broken a rib. Unlike most girls I liked mosh pits. I was into banging into people and I didn't mind getting whacked by flailing limbs. It was like a switch got flipped in my head and I just went nuts dancing. I was what I guess you would call a punk although it was really more a lifestyle than my haircut or what we think of as punks now. To me being a punk was not caring. I was very good at not caring. There was a book we had when we were kids in which there is a boy named Pierre who says nothing but "I don't care." Eventually he gets eaten by a lion and burped up and then finally he cares. But I wasn't there yet. So I just did stuff, lived with people, slept with people, hitchhiked with people. It was actually a very relaxing way to live if you compare it to my current situation. I was walking down Thirty-fourth Street in Manhattan—my couch for the night was a couple blocks away—and I saw a pair of army boots in the window of the Army Recruitment Office. I had really been wanting a pair, the hard black leather kind, but I couldn't afford them. So I stopped to admire the ones in the window. I was still just a tiny bit drunk. I made money at a record store in those days, but not enough to buy boots, so I had to wear sneakers with my fishnet tights and that made me feel like a boob. The longer I stood there in front of the Army Recruitment Office, the more special those boots became. There was something about those boots. I mean they were special. Looking back on it, I think that what made them so special was you were allowed to kill in them. The army was in fact inviting you to kill in them should the need arise. But I didn't see that at the time. I wasn't really thinking. I wanted to sit down in front of someone who would tell me what to do. I wanted someone to take care of me a little, give me some advice. Oh fuck it. You want to know? I'll tell you. I wanted free boots. So I enlisted in the army.

I didn't tell my friends my plan. I started doing push-ups, pull-ups, and running along the East River. I took the ASVAB test, it was not too hard. I signed the six-year contract to join the army. Then I packed what the army said I needed in a duffel bag, put the rest in a black garbage bag, and left it with the friends whose couch I had last slept on. Then there was the long, long, silent bus ride to Fort Jackson, pulling up in the dark, our drill sergeant sticking his head into the bus yelling at us to get off. As I stood in line holding my paperwork in one hand and my duffel in the other, the sergeant said to me, "Ma'am, I recommend you fix your face because you need to make your attitude less visible." I thought that it was interesting he didn't want me to change my attitude, just make it less visible. Then he told us to give him some push-ups and as I did those he said something I loved: "We make it so you do not have to think. We tell you everything you need to know. We tell you the whos, the whats, the wheres, and the whens." I stood up and dusted myself off and the sergeant said, "If I wanted you to dust yourself off, I would have told you."

I met my husband in the army. Once when I was setting out the pizza on a ping-pong table at Fort Jackson, he came up behind me and pretended to hump me and all the guys laughed. That was embarrassing but I could take a joke. There was a lot of razzing then for the women. When we were deployed, JP and I didn't see each other for a few years. when we met up again I reminded him about the fun at the ping-pong table and he had forgotten. He liked my ginger-head hair and matching pubic patch. Brown eyes. A fairly big wide nose. I look like my mother and she was French. Some men prefer plain girls who, from a distance, seem pretty. Or if you squint. I did fine in the army.

I have not gotten dressed in six days. I can't decide what to wear. I do shower though. I shower and get back into my nightgown. In a way it just seems more practical. Then you're ready for bed. I think I am a little depressed, though what I really fear is that I am getting incredibly boring. Just so boring that I have no outer sign for the world left. No interest whatsoever. I have nothing to say to people anymore. They ask me how I am at the grocery store and I say fine and then the conversation just hangs there. I see the end of the exchange, I see how it's going to come out, and so, having had it in advance, I just decide not to have it. Like getting dressed. I know I am going to have to get undressed again so why get dressed. I have become mercilessly logical.

Christ is Mercy. He sees the rotten stinking parts of us, the pus and so on, and says I love you anyway my son. My daughter. In my case I do not think I have much pus. I think I have a beige nubbly interior, sort of like the exterior of this typewriter. It's true I have thoughts—violent thoughts. But they don't belong to me. They appear in my mind like a pride of lions in an empty shopping mall. I glare at them with the frigid scorn of a gleaming Coke machine. They pad up still escalators, sniff at barren popcorn stalls, they lick sticky remains of ice cream off shining stone floors. They shit in the planters. And when they go, when the automatic doors close behind them, they leave no trace, only a few gigantic turds around the trunks of the plastic trees. These turds are the shadows of my thoughts. And this is where my problem lies: I am clotted with shit. I knew a girl. She was the daughter of an artist that lived nearby. I used to play in her house. She had long brown frizzy hair. Once we were walking down the hill away from her house and she froze, grabbing my hand. "What is it?" I asked. "I just saw God," she said. She didn't elaborate, but I believed her. She was very bossy. I liked it though. I enjoy crawling into someone else's hand and letting them rattle me around like a single die. I saw her recently. Brought my kids over to her house. She isn't married. She makes twenty-foot steel sculptures that look like enormous red fingernails glued together. She was really happy to see me and the girls at first but then after a while I could tell we were boring her. She wanted to get back to the studio. She had a commission. I envied her. Not for the commission—for believing it was important. For believing in anything enough to devote your whole life to it, get up at six in the morning and slave away till one, have a meager slice of bread and cheese and then go back to work, fighting against fatigue and back strain—struggling to get the thing done in time for the big unveiling. And then it's a pile of giant fingernails. The only thing I feel proud of is my kids. I know I don't have the right—they came out just the same as they are now. All I did was prevent them from dying of exposure or hunger. Ellen emerged fighting, red-faced, furious. Wendy came out relaxed, curious, gentle. And that's the way they are now. They are my pride and joy and they're the reason I get dressed, when I did used to get dressed. Of course I will have to go food shopping, and that's today. I can't keep giving JP lists. I think he stays with me because I don't need him anymore. I don't seem to need him because I don't speak. Talking only leads to misunderstandings. Silence is perfect. I am afraid I will say something pungent. A stink will come out of my mouth. This makes it impossible to answer the phone,

which drives JP crazy. But to get back to my subject. Of
the little moment when I went the wrong way, from prom-
ising young woman to flotsam, to extraneousness—like
the strands that rub off a ribbon and that you cut away.
sometime last year it hit me nothing was safe. It started
with driving. I was on 9G which has a 55-mile-an-hour
speed limit which is on the fast side in my opinion anyway
which I have always felt but this time as I was driving
there was this truck coming toward me exactly the same
make as my own truck which is a Chevy and the same
color which is white, and I was sure it was going to swerve
and hit me. I got paralyzed with the sense of the inevita-
bility of it and just got ready to die. When the truck passed
without hitting me, it didn't really help. I swerved off the
road and parked on the dirt shoulder for a long time.
Sweat was all down my sides and I couldn't breathe full
breaths, just little half-breaths. I started crying, too, this
panicked out-of-body crying. Like it was someone else
crying. There were no thoughts attached. It was physical,
and sort of animal. I had stopped being a person and I
was just fear. So from then on my point of view sort of
shifted and I was no longer in any way relaxed. which is
funny because here's what got no reaction whatsoever
from me: I was driving in a convoy of armored vehicles
driving out of Kabul. There was a flash ahead of us and
a detonation. I saw an arm floating by my window—very
slow, like it was moving through water. They treated all
the soldiers in our armored vehicle for PTSD because of
what we had seen, but of all of us, I was the one who was
most fine. They say there can be a delayed reaction. Who

knows. I did find out there was a therapist who took my insurance locally and went and sat in the man's chair and he said a few things that made me think he was an idiot. Plus I couldn't really speak because of the problem of the potential stench coming out of my mouth. I am turning to stone is what it is. I need silence and solitude. If everyone could just stop talking for five minutes I could gather myself. If JP would stop asking me if I'm okay, and the kids. I am very sorry about the kids.

I joined a new church. It is a tiny church and there are few people who go. It's next to a cornfield. I started taking the kids. JP wouldn't be caught dead there, he's a Methodist and this is a severe and true Catholic church for Charismatic Catholics which is as hardcore as you can get really. Here is what gets me, Lord: how you let us all just be so lost, how you let events pile up in a person's life and push them one way or the other and then in the end they get pushed right off the edge. How are we meant to protect our children from all the bad things, all the danger, all the murderous psychos and the war and the accidents. It got so I wouldn't let them out of the house, and I wouldn't send them to school. JP would go to work and I would say goodbye and then keep them home all day. There was one school bus that went on fire and all the children burned. I was up all night thinking about that. I felt like something terrible is going to happen anyway so maybe get it over with now when they are sleeping. I just need it to be quiet. Now I am here and they are upstairs and they are not in this world anymore but the next. They get to be happy and pure and saved and I am condemned to walk the earth with the mark of Cain on my forehead. Everyone will know I have done what no one can do. Very few. I asked so many times for God to save me and purify my thoughts, to give me even five minutes of respite. But God was silent. He didn't say anything or extend any mercy on me. Silent and smug, the smugness of total power and total indifference. And now here I am and I

Joad stared at the letters on the page until they began to dissolve and float. Then she put the two leaves of onionskin paper back together and tried to fold them up. Her fingers felt clumsy, their movements approximate. Giving up, she stuffed the pages back into her shirt pocket, thinking, "That's why the house was so cheap."

In the middle of the night, Joad whipped off the covers and stood; the room slanted. She gripped the wall, confused. Delicately, she made her way to the bathroom, legs planted wide. From the toilet, she observed a gentle floating of the light switch, with the cracked drywall around it, inexpertly painted by her or Andrew, she could not remember. Staggering back into the bedroom, she felt for the mattress and let herself fall onto it.

"Ow!" said Andrew. "This is me here. I exist."

"I'm dizzy," she said.

"Go back to sleep," he said, gathering her in a pile of bedding and kissing her ear. Joad thought about the woman who wrote the letter. That woman had emerged from the secretary desk and grabbed her by the throat. She could sense a malign force in the room. She imagined blood on the walls, kids screaming. Andrew slept without knowing. She could never tell him. It would break his heart. She felt her secret suffocating her.

Joad woke to a world somehow unreal. She felt spacey and disconnected. She did what work she could, and in the late afternoon, she made focaccia, wrapped it in a tea towel, cut a bouquet of zinnias from the flower patch, and followed the shoulder of the road to Colleen's, passing through the open gate. As she rounded the side of the big river house, she remembered the hysterical dog and stopped. She looked up at the porch, which was already bathed in golden light. And there, sure enough, was Colleen.

"Hi!" said Joad, waving. "I made focaccia, I thought you might like some. And . . ." Her voice trailed off as she saw Colleen flop one leg off her recliner, make a move to stand, then drop back again.

"I'll come back," said Joad.

"No, no. You come up here."

"I really didn't want to barge in, I'll just leave these here." She lay the bread and flowers on the top step and turned to go.

"Siddown," said Colleen. "Please." Joad sat down opposite Colleen, her back to the sunset. Colleen was wearing an aged pair of peach-colored sweatpants and a stained white T-shirt that read LOBSTER HEAVEN. Her gray hair was stringy and unwashed. She looked like her own alcoholic twin.

"So." Colleen stared at Joad, her creased face deflated. "I am fascinated by you, I don't mind saying, Joad."

"I don't think of myself as all that interesting."

"All that history you carry around in you."

"I don't know much about it, really."

"You should do some research. You could learn something about yourself. Drink?" Joad glanced at the bottle of white wine on the floor.

"Um . . . maybe white wine?"

"In the fridge. This one's dead. Go back and back."

Joad kicked off her sandals as she entered the house, walking onto a plush carpet, and looked around for a way to the kitchen. Two grimy yellow couches, a large painting of a horse, a terra-cotta sculpture of a young woman's head on the glass coffee table . . . "Back and back!" bellowed Colleen from outside. At the far end of the room, a red hallway opened into the dim distance, and Joad followed it. Its walls were hung with framed photographs, hundreds of them, arranged from floor to ceiling higgledy-piggledy, a whole big life. Joad wanted to stop and look at each and every picture, to snoop and snoop. She took in a few images as she walked: Colleen in her sixties laughing with Bill Clinton; Colleen the large-scale American beauty posing on the porch with her two blond sons. One of them was clearly Trevor, his head tilted, hurt smile on his face. Colleen's husband had been handsome, dark, a little portly, a cigar in his hand as he held forth. Colleen sitting confidently on a desk in a pantsuit, her fair hair sleek, glasses on her head. "Go back and back," Colleen had said. How far could this hallway go? Joad time-traveled through Trevor's birth, Chet as a puppy, or rather an earlier version of Chet, a city soiree where a mid-twenties Colleen was an absolute knockout in black silk, standing beside—was that James Baldwin?—and then, a young Colleen, fifteen or so, towheaded, running along the beach, her solid legs a blur as she cantered toward all that promise in the hall. Having come to more or less the beginning, Joad was birthed into the kitchen, where an old white fridge stood humbly in the corner. Joad opened the door to find numerous bottles of white wine, a nest of ineffectually rewrapped cheeses, and a cloudy tub of hummus. She grabbed a bottle and trotted back down the hall, her head down, ignoring the photos.

When she got to the porch, Colleen was grooming a recumbent Chet, raking a brush down the dog's broad flank, releasing big greasy puffs of white dog hair into the air. The puffs would blow a little distance, then catch themselves on a chair leg or get trapped in a corner. Without looking up, Colleen pointed to a low sideboard.

"Glasses over there." Joad took a glass, filled it, and refilled Colleen's. Colleen sat back and took a sip.

"What did you say you brought?"

"Focaccia. Want some?"

"Sure." Joad brought over the bread. Colleen unwrapped it and tore off a hunk with her teeth.

"Mmm." Joad looked away, waiting for the ravenous chewing to subside.

"Do you . . . remember the people who farmed our place before us?"

"The last people to really farm that land were the Leavenworths. But the last brother died and they sold it to—I don't remember the name. A Catholic family. And then *they* sold it to Fiona."

"Fiona?"

"Fiona Donovan. She raised miniature horses. She was a hoarder and hadn't lived in it for years when she sold it to Trevor, which explains the state it was in when you bought it." Colleen drained her glass and poured herself another. On her cheek, by her ear, was a bruise.

"Are you okay?"

"Hm?"

Joad touched her own face where Colleen's bruise was.

"Oh, it's nothing, I think I knocked into something. It's sore when I touch it. So I don't." Irritated by the sympathy, Colleen looked into the distance, sullen.

"She was a curious little thing. To look at her she seemed utterly banal."

"Fiona?" Colleen nodded.

"Did something happen with her . . . an accident, in our house?"

"An *accident*?" said Colleen, emphasizing the word as though it were an insane notion.

"With her children."

"What in the world are you talking about? Fiona didn't

47

have any children. I wish she had, maybe she would have left me alone."

"What did she do to you?"

"She hounded me. You see, I was in publishing for a great many years. I was an editor. We lived in the city and came out here for weekends. Then about a thousand years ago, I retired, and since then I have been a permanent resident. And now I detest the weekend people."

"But what did Fiona want from you?"

"To be published! She was desperate to be a writer. She wrote and she wrote. Story after story, all about women living around here. And every one of them ended up in my mailbox. She was relentless. Truth is, Fiona started to scare me after a while . . ." Joad stared at Colleen, not listening anymore.

A writer! What a dirty trick. Walking away from the river house, Joad felt as though reading the typed pages had infected her with a virus that she had to carry around now, nasty images downloaded into her head. What a weird thing reading is. For a time, that woman who killed her children had been so real to her, and now she wasn't. Their house was clean again. But still the images remained. Fiona Donovan. People were such mysteries. Joad thought about Colleen, drunk and alone on her porch with Chet, her glory days hanging in the hallway, watching the indifferent sunset. Joad wondered how she'd gotten that bruise. If there was something wrong. A hawk glided overhead. It seemed too big. Maybe it was an eagle. Joad crested the hill and turned to their field. The many rows of vegetables were exact and abundant, a tumult of growth bursting out of that black soil. This is real, she marveled. This exists.

She entered the house. It was cool. She shivered beneath her T-shirt. Peering into the room off the kitchen, she saw that Andrew had lugged the secretary desk in there for her, along with a kitchen chair. Joad walked into the bright little space. She sat down at the desk and took in the boxes of seeds, her recipe notebooks stacked along the walls. She anticipated the pleasure of organizing this room. Joad stroked the smooth top of the desk with her hardened brown hands, feeling the grain with her fingertips. She imagined herself growing old at this desk. She imagined leaving it to her child. Leaning down, she rested her cheek on the cool wood, inhaled the rich, heady scent of beeswax, and heard herself whisper,

"You're mine."

VAPORS

Justine was pushing Francis in his stroller along the New York City sidewalk. She looked down at his sand-colored curls ruffled by the breeze as he leaned back, one ankle crossed over his knee, his bottle in his mouth, gazing out at the world in a state of trusting relaxation as he sucked contemplatively at his rice milk. She crossed Prince Street, trying to remember where that café was. She and Francis had an hour to kill before his music class, and she craved a cappuccino. She was about to get to the curb, had lifted the front wheels of the stroller, when she heard her name. She turned toward the voice and there he was, standing there, like Death. His beauty was staggering, and she felt herself, though very slightly, stagger.

"Hi, Joseph," she said. What else was she supposed to say.

"I thought it was you."

"Well, it is."

"Then I thought it couldn't be."

"Why not?"

"Who is *this*?"

"This is Francis."

"Saint Francis."

"No, just Francis."

Joseph chortled. He was wearing a pair of black jeans. Maybe the same black jeans he'd owned years ago, the ones she was so familiar with. Likewise the black turtleneck, even in this heat. His uniform. The round eyes rimmed with dark circles stared out of his alabaster face. Vampire football hero had always been his look.

"Do you live around here?" he asked.

"I'm here for work," she said.

"I heard you moved away."

"I did," she said. "Are you . . . still in your same apartment?"

"Yes."

The apartment on Avenue C startled her with its nearness then. She could smell the enormous cat, Sweeney, and the unwashed linoleum floors. She had a memory of lying on those grubby tiles with Joseph, the first time. He told her she was beautiful on the inside.

They had been introduced by her dad's friend Anouk, an experimental filmmaker in her fifties. Joseph wrote Justine a postcard after that encounter, asking if she wanted to get coffee and talk, that he was "around if you ever need an ear." As though he was willing to do her a favor. She was intrigued, but coffee with Joseph was complicated by the fact that Justine had recently moved back in with her college boyfriend, Elliot. She and Elliot had lived together after college for a couple of years. They fought with the clean, absolute rage of siblings, pulverizing their sex life while ballooning their mutual affection to a point where they seemed destined to be together;

their breakup was incomplete, shadowed by the specter of marriage in the offing, despite all the evidence. Their solution to this conundrum was to find an apartment with a three-month lease. That is, they wanted to try living together again, but not for a whole year. This apartment was on Lafayette Street. They never actually had any sex there, and Elliot always seemed to be agreeing to babysit his brother Seth's ancient dog in White Plains, because Seth was an emergency room doctor whose girlfriend had left him, the dog needed a lot of attention, and the ex-girlfriend had no interest in sharing custody of an epileptic Weimaraner. A few weeks into the lease, Justine, who was a fashion photographer, booked a job in L.A.; the fashion house put her up at a trendy hotel where she was given a nice sunny apartment with a kitchen. It made her feel so happy to be in that little apartment with no memories. In need of a book, she dashed across Sunset Boulevard during a pause in the traffic and ran into the bookshop facing the hotel. After browsing in the history section, then the fiction section, she decided on a biography of Barbara Stanwyck. She loved Barbara Stanwyck as an actress and was anxious to know the details of her life. She opened the book while she was on line to pay and was already fascinated when she heard her old name. "Tiny?" She looked up and there behind the register was her first boyfriend ever, Hal, from boarding school. She hadn't seen him in nearly ten years.

"Hal," she said. "How weird." Hal had been the only person ever so far to break Justine's heart, when she was seventeen, because of a transgression. You might call it Justine's *ur*-transgression.

Justine had gone to boarding school because her bereaved

and distracted father, when she was in tenth grade, suddenly realized that her public school had no arts program, and limited science. At boarding school, she quickly caught up on all she hadn't learned in her small rural high school about hard drugs and sex. She got to affect a whole new identity. She was "Tiny," the rough-edged girl from public school who smoked unfiltered cigarettes and rarely spoke. She met Hal when she was fifteen and he was seventeen. He was her first love. After a year, Hal graduated and went to college. One day that fall, her scofflaw roommate Kelsey, irritated by Justine's virginity, arranged for Hal to sneak into Justine's dorm room and sleep there overnight. It all worked according to plan, but right after the awkward act, which felt to Justine like trying to mount a baseball bat, there was a bang on her door, and they were busted. Justine was suspended and placed on final warning (Hal just took the train back to college). She remained faithful to Hal all senior year, becoming in fact a famous cocktease, but the night before graduation she got tipsy and had a big flirt with Kelsey's younger brother, whom she had only met that night. She went on a family dinner with Kelsey's wealthy family, was somehow served a great deal of wine at the restaurant, and ended up with her foot in the brother's crotch under the table. After the dinner, as Kelsey's father drove them all back to the dorm, Justine, sandwiched between Kelsey and Kelsey's cousin, Didi, who was also in their class, kissed the brother sloppily in the back of the car, and happened to be sitting on his lap in the common room when Hal walked into her dorm, smiling and windswept, having hitchhiked all the way from Amherst—or maybe she was making up the hitchhiking—but definitely having made a big effort to see her graduate. And there she was on this kid's lap. Hal looked so shocked when he saw her. She had been bad and traitorous and bad and she didn't know why. The next morning, she dragged herself over to the boys' dorm where Hal was staying, feeling nauseous, and pleaded with him to forgive her. He didn't seem angry, but he wasn't friendly, either; he was scarily neutral. Justine really hated herself for having made such a stupid mistake and hurting Hal, and she just hated herself, but she still had to put on the pretty linen graduation dress her father had found her, with a sailor's collar on it trimmed in blue and a big blue bow on the back. She looked so innocent in the dress, yet she felt like an absolute monster. After that, Hal didn't trust her anymore, and although she came to visit him a few times in New York City where he was working over the summer, things were not the same between them; one day at a diner, Hal launched into a very long, awkward sentence that Justine began to realize was going to end with a breakup, so she stood up, stricken, walked out the door, and began a season of heartsickness that lasted through her first semester of college.

Now, here was Hal, a decade later, standing behind the cash register at the bookstore on Sunset. They exchanged a few words and arranged to meet the following day. That night, she got a call from a recent ex-boyfriend, Carlos, who was in L.A. working as an electrician on a TV show. She spent the afternoon at her fashion shoot photographing extremely tall, surreally beautiful women, and by the end of the day she felt like a garden gnome. She answered Carlos's call enthusiastically and they had sex in her apartment without memories in the trendy hotel, only now there was a memory in it, which was of having sex with Carlos standing up in the kitchen. She and Carlos had been together for two years and broken up really because she'd been unfaithful to him with a charismatic older friend named Larry, who had bad diabetes and was missing several toes. Larry was a real physical mess and Justine got naked with him more out of a sense of friendliness than anything—and maybe curiosity—but either way she should not have mentioned this to Carlos, obviously. But to be fair Carlos already knew she had a problem with fidelity; their affair started when she was working as a set photographer on a low-budget picture he was on the crew of. She was going out with another photographer at the time, Ben, who was so upset when he realized she was sleeping with Carlos that he moved to Pittsburgh. Anyway, when Carlos left the hotel, she called Elliot, with whom if you remember she was still living in their three-month-lease apartment on Lafayette Street. Elliot said something like, "Getting back together with you is easier than I expected." By which he meant she was easy to get along with in her absence. Justine laughed at this, not pausing to think about what her life was becoming.

The following day she worked until six, then met Hal in an outdoor place where they shared guacamole. There was this sweetness between them, an echo of extreme youth. He drove her to basically a flophouse where he was renting a bare room, saving every penny till he made it as an actor. He really was beautiful, with long, slender arms and those legs that she had always called "fried chicken legs" when they were kids because they were tanned with blond hairs all over them that made her think of glistening grease. He told her how weird it was that she had turned up at the bookstore like that because in the past year he had started thinking of her a lot and regretting how they had parted. The next few days she was over at his room often, talking and doing a little kissing, but they didn't make love. They just reminisced about the past and stared into each other's eyes. Hal claimed that he didn't want to be with Justine physically unless they were together as a couple, because he was in love with her and he would be too hurt if it didn't work out. So now, here she was, wallowing in nostalgia with Hal in his flophouse while Elliot waited in the three-month apartment for her to get back to the nostalgia she felt for him and their days in college. She was trapped in a kaleidoscope of nostalgia. She returned to New York and the confusion continued. She and Elliot shared hilarious dinners and then went to bed and stared at the ceiling. Hal flew east to see his mother but also to be with Justine. He invited her to go to his mother Sybil's house near Rochester. Justine knew Sybil from the days she and Hal went out in boarding school and she had come upstate for the weekend, Sybil banging on the locked door of Hal's room yelling, "Do-not-get-that-girl-pregnant!" as Justine read *One Flew Over the Cuckoo's Nest* on Hal's bed, fully clothed. But Sybil did have a point.

Justine knew if she went to Hal's mother's house this would be a statement that she and Hal were going to be together. She could not decide whether to go or not. Elliot was at his brother's house in White Plains babysitting the palsied dog for the weekend and she spent an afternoon in an agony of indecision. Then, as she wondered what to do, she found herself packing her bag to go visit Hal at his mother's place; that was how she discovered what she had decided.

Hal's mother, a hulking landscape gardener, had always gotten along with Justine, but also suspected her of being a little tough for her son. The first evening after dinner, Sybil took out her computer to show off Hal's big acting break in a long-running cop series. Hal tried to prevent this, but he didn't try too hard, so he and Justine sat folded up together on the couch, his arm around her, and they all watched the episode, in which Hal played a weepy heroin addict. He had three highly emotional scenes—screaming scenes, crying scenes. Watching him, Justine could tell he wasn't really feeling anything. He was just screwing up his face. It was fakery. She kept trying to tell herself it shouldn't matter—that there was something wrong with her if it mattered so much. Yet, despite her wishes, she felt a shovel full of ash fall gently over her bright heart, extinguishing it. The next day, she took the train back to the city, sat down with Elliot, and poured a glass of wine. You'd think this whole clusterfuck would end here, but no.

Justine took the bus home to Connecticut to visit her father, a melancholic yet gregarious Frenchman, and her father's Serbian girlfriend Behida. Justine's mother had died when she was twelve, and Behida had been around for the past few years, which was a relief because her father had been inconsolable after the death of his wife. The minute Justine got home, she went upstairs to her old room and fell asleep on top of the bed. She woke to a spectral body of light glimmering on the pink ceiling. She looked out the window and there was dusk happening all across the lawn, golden rays strewn over the trees like great webs. She took her old Leica outside and started snapping. Eventually, a car drove up; she recognized her father's friend Anouk exiting the car. Anouk waved at Justine, her bracelets jangling. Then this guy around Justine's age got out of the car, too. He was all in black, tall, broad-shouldered, pallid. "This is Joseph," said Anouk. "He's writing the new screenplay with me."

Justine's father had a passion for dinner parties. He and Behida hosted them all the time. There was always loud talk over the table and lots of wine flowing, and Justine's small father would hold forth one paragraph at a time, pointing the tip of his tongue out of his mouth to reset, then launch on another paragraph, expounding on French film, or maybe Swedish or Finnish film. He owned a small art house cinema, and film was the great passion of his life. Justine was sat beside Joseph at the dinner. They talked about photography, mostly. He was a photographer as well as a writer. He was earnest and respectful. That was when he asked for her mailing address, which she found quaint. And two days later the postcard arrived, with the offer to listen.

A few weeks after the disaster at Hal's mother's house, Justine found the postcard at the bottom of her bag, covered in crumbs. She called Joseph and they went out for lunch, took a subway up to MoMA, drifted past some artwork, walked sixty blocks down to the Lower East Side and toured the Tenement Museum, then had falafel for dinner on a bench. The date lasted eight hours. Joseph was deeply interested in Justine. She found herself opening up to him, telling him all about Elliot, the sadness she felt at the fading of that big relationship, the confusion of thinking she had been in love with Hal and then realizing she had been mistaken. She talked about her work, how grateful she was to get fashion jobs, even as she wondered if she should be doing more political work. Joseph listened as no one had ever listened to her before. Often, his eyes were trained on the ground as she spoke, as if he were visualizing her words, and he nodded slowly. Days later, when he showed her his work on his computer, she was relieved and intimidated. He was really good. He shot still lifes of fruit, vases, sometimes a dead bird—classic themes with an eerie quality. Shot on black-and-white film, the images were overexposed, silvery; the presence of dead animals and skulls hinted at a gothic core. A few days later, she went to his apartment. That's where Justine met Joseph's massive cat, Sweeney, and spent some quality time on the floor.

Soon, the three-month lease with Elliot was up. They both sobbed, and they were both relieved. Elliot moved in with his brother temporarily and Justine walked around Little Italy till she found a man sweeping outside a building. She asked him if he knew of any apartments around there; he took a good look at her, showed her a place upstairs, and she wrote out a check.

Soon, Justine and Joseph were a couple. Joseph supported himself as a bartender in a restaurant uptown. Justine had a small inheritance from her mother, which she used whenever she was between photography jobs. Joseph had no such cushion. His father was a lineman for the telephone company. Joseph came to Justine's apartment in Little Italy every night after work with a tub of salad from what he called the "sneeze bar" of the local deli. He ate his salad drenched in French dressing. She had convinced him to stop eating burgers every night. He spent a lot of time in his black turtleneck, naked from the waist down.

Joseph started photographing Justine unclad in his apartment, as part of his still life series, with grapes on her stomach, or curled up on a platter of raw sausages. Sometimes Sweeney was in the photos, her massive form hunched, cross face pointed to the camera.

The first time Joseph was a little bit mean to Justine, they were on the beach in Far Rockaway. As they walked along, talking, Joseph threw sand in Justine's face. She laughed and threw sand at him, but then he did it again, and again, and again. She felt as she had when she was a child and other children had bullied her. It was a confusing moment. She tried to smile. Maybe the fact that Justine had been bullied as a child made her the perfect partner for Joseph. But whatever the reason for her tolerance, she looked back on that day on the beach as the beginning of everything else. There was a slight bondage-y aspect to the sex, but that was really nothing compared to the bondage of everyday life.

He started to say things in a jocular tone, like, "I am going to hit you so hard your jaw is hanging by a thread." Or, "I would like to serve you a little espresso cup of shit." He pointed out some physical flaws she had not yet noticed, such as her lack of a real ass, and called her breasts "big old droopy milk wagons" in a jokey, confusing voice. He also disparaged her photography, after a time. He told her that her mushy, middle-class, pretentious upbringing made it impossible for her ever to do great work, that only working-class people had ever done anything worthwhile. He recited lists to prove it. She felt he was right. He told her that her work was clearly made by a female, that it was girls' pictures. He had heard from someone working on a shoot with her that she was not highly regarded by the crew. He taught her how to cull her images mercilessly, disregarding all but the best. He had a great eye. She no longer trusted her own judgment, and constantly asked him to review her selects. Then one day he wondered out loud why Justine's father had allowed her mother to be cared for by strangers in a hospice at the end of her life, something she had confided to him. Justine said she thought it was because he was afraid of making a mistake with her care. Joseph said it was typical middle-class coldness, an inability to face real life. And this was a terrible thing to contemplate, because Justine's father had avoided her mother in the last months—however much he loved her, he delegated her to strangers at the humiliating end, popping in to hold her hand once a day and make a few cheerful remarks, unable to face what was happening. It was a moral failure that Joseph had laid bare. One by one, with amazing efficiency, operating entirely by instinct, Joseph was removing the things that had made Justine believe in herself. And she allowed him to do this, allowed it like a person whose home is broken into and watches, silent and afraid, as all their valuables are taken. Sometimes, Joseph could be very kind, nearly angelic. In these moments, Justine loved him absolutely. It was as though she had been bewitched, all her strength sapped away.

One curious thing was, Justine was no longer unfaithful. Of this she had been cured. And one day it happened that from dawn until dusk, she wept, and then the next day, too, and the next. She felt she was dissolving, like a lozenge in the rain. She didn't mind so much. It was Elliot, by now married, who told her father what was happening to Justine. Her father took her to stay with relatives in France for three months, and she remained there, moving to Paris and finding work as a portrait photographer through a family friend. She thought about Joseph all the time in the beginning. It was like an ache, an addiction. It was the first time she'd been without a guy since she was fifteen. Yet she found a grim pleasure in her solitude. She feasted on work for a couple of years, taking any photography job she could find, and rose gradually up the ladder of prestige to the point where she was shooting ad campaigns and some editorial for fashion magazines. One spring, she was booked for a major fashion shoot in the Garde Républicaine, an immured garrison on Boulevard Henri IV. The story would be splashy, with photos of the handsome gendarmes in their gold Napoleonic helmets alongside models in evening gowns. Justine got to the Garde Républicaine an hour before the appointed time with a single camera, to get a sense of the light. Her assistant for the day would bring the rest of the gear. She walked through the high, baroque stone archway of the entrance. Three mounted policemen practiced jumps in the center of the sunny courtyard. To her right, a square doorway led to the stables. As she entered, Justine smelled dung and hay, her eyes adjusting to the darkness. Scanty light fell from high, semicircular windows. The horses were largely turned away, blanketed behind the iron bars of their stalls, eating oats from small metal troughs set into the stone walls. Justine noticed a man at the end of the long room, standing on a crate, holding the bridle of a massive black horse tight as he trained a pinprick of light into its eye. Instinctively, Justine stalked the image. With a light tread she approached the scene, raising her camera. Through the lens she could now discern the man's expression of absorbed concentration, his angular face resting against the horse's dark muzzle as he pointed the needle of light into its wild, frightened eye. Justine pressed the shutter. The man looked down, spooked, and released the horse's halter. Justine explained herself, apologizing for startling him. Blushing, he stepped down from the crate and introduced himself. Étienne was the veterinarian for the horses of the Garde Républicaine. Justine asked in her homely French about the animal he was treating now. He explained it had a cataract. This man had a manner new to Justine: self-effacing, yet steeped in his own competence. Justine asked him if she could take another picture. Reluctant, shy, he allowed it. She asked him to take a step to his left, into the light. He missed the mark. Without thinking, she reached out to adjust him. As her fingers brushed his bare forearm, a shock branched out through her hand and her body, causing a sudden and profound ache in her womb. Within six months, she was pregnant with Francis and had moved into Étienne's small but charming apartment in the barracks of the Garde Républicaine.

Francis swiveled in his stroller and looked up at his mother, his dark almond-shaped eyes inquisitive, wispy little eyebrows raised. He wondered why she had stopped pushing him, but also, possibly, more. Francis was a gifted, wise, rather serious person, even though he was only two. Often, he looked at Justine with an encouraging smile, as if to say, "You are going to be all right." She was not imagining it. He really did look at her that way. And now he was saying, "Perhaps we had better go."

"We have to go," said Justine.

"Already?" said Joseph, flaring his nostrils slightly and raising his chin, as if trying to puff himself up with his former power.

"Bye!" she said.

"Goodbye, Justine." He took her hand and shook it, his expression at once solemn and ironic.

Justine pushed the stroller to the café she intended to go to, heart hammering, and entered. Sitting down, she pulled Francis onto her lap, sniffing him behind his ear, where it smelled like a fresh roll, and waited for the tide of feeling for Joseph to come in—regret, love, rage, desire. She kept scanning herself, but there was nothing. She felt nothing at all for Joseph anymore! She had nearly died from love of him and now it was all just empty images. For so long she had yearned for the pain to go away, and now that it had, she found it chilling. Why bother feeling so much in life if it all turns to vapor? She cast her gaze down at Francis, at his round cheek as he tried to replace the cap of his bottle with a chubby hand, the curls near his neck humid with sweat, then out the window of the café, at the people passing—all these strangers who were in love, or abandoned, or desperate, or happy. "It will pass," she warned them silently, the heat of Francis's back against her belly.

TOTAL

They had planned to name her Eva, but after she was born, they always referred to her as E.

Looking back now, it's hard to comprehend how powerful the Total Phone was.

People who have used one equate the experience to being injected with heroin, or perhaps what a baby feels when breastfeeding. A feeling of complete warmth and acceptance surrounded each Total Phone encounter like a nimbus. The phone was a mind-melder. It dissolved the barrier between the two people on the call.

Some people reached orgasm, though for most it was more of a spiritual sensation, first signaled by a tingling at the top of the head and a feeling of heat rushing through the body. The religious claimed it was what Adam and Eve must have felt before the Fall.

The first, primitive models of the Total Phone were like old-fashioned phone booths you had to enter. These were prohibitively expensive. Later, a force field was created that the caller could enter with a few taps on the phone's keypad. The phones were still very pricey, but there were plenty of people who could buy them. It is now agreed that it was the force fields that caused the chromosomal changes in the embryos.

Only the rich had been able to afford Total Phones; only the idle could afford the obsession the device engendered. To have a Total child was a strange sort of status symbol.

Children with Total Syndrome had triangular, arrow-shaped skulls. Their eyes were in the highest quadrant of their heads, near the corners. Their features were relatively flat. They had tiny mouths and developed tiny teeth. Postmortems revealed that there were no adult teeth waiting to come down behind the milk teeth in Total babies. Nature knew better than that. Their skin was very smooth. They had an expressionless affect. They blinked slowly. Although they were not able to learn language, Totals often seemed to be thinking, and could learn repetitive actions. They were easily toilet trained and seemed to be naturally neat. They often displayed evidence of apparently random emotion. Despite their difference in aspect from normal humans, Total children had a doll-like appeal.

There were entrepreneurs from New York to Shanghai who were swift to take advantage of the need to care for the Totals. Total hospitals. Total training schools. Total Management. Total Care. Total Waldorf. All of these systems were palliative, each distinctly emphasizing comfort and distraction, lacking in hope. They were warehouses in which to deposit these seemingly identical, docile children—places where they would be cared for as long as they lived. Total children had short life spans. A female in Iceland had lived to the age of twelve, but as a rule the children died by age eight or nine.

The cause of death was never apparent. They simply ran down and expired like batteries.

The parents, already caved in with guilt about bringing on this illness through their own decadent fascination with an unnecessary object, often could not bring themselves to love a child doomed to die before its tenth birthday. Plus, the Totals were so prone to allergies and infection. They needed twenty-four-hour care.

There were support groups.

Total Phones were, of course, taken off the market once the connection was proven, but not before thousands of toxic conceptions and hundreds of lawsuits. For years after the babies started being born, the company denied the assertions of the parents as "bad science" and kept fabricating the phones. The demand was enormous despite the risks. Total Phones were more addictive than cigarettes.

But all that feels like ancient history now. The last Total died twenty years ago. Since then, Total Care Centers have been repurposed to cater to victims of other diseases. Some have become apartment complexes. Others stand empty, their hivelike structures populated by flying squirrels and snakes. Teenagers use them to smoke and fuck in. Junkies shoot up there.

But in that period, the wealthy world was gripped with terror for a good few years. It's hard to imagine the fear experienced by a woman who had used a Total Phone and then found out she was pregnant. Total Syndrome was very difficult to detect in utero, because a balloonlike sac developed around the baby's head, in the shape of a normal head, with a yolk inside it that looked like a normal brain. Few mothers would abort a fetus on the off chance it was abnormal. Least of all my mother.

The day had just turned cloudy. Irritated, I pulled my sweatshirt over my damp bathing suit. I hated the cool air on my hot skin. The sea was now the color of lead; a breeze was picking up. I looked over at my mother. She was lying on her stomach, reading, oblivious to the change in temperature. I put my camera up to my eye, pointed it down at her, and tried to find a frame. Her short, white-blond hair was stringy from seawater; sand coated her back. I shifted the lens toward the sea and found my father trudging along the beach, ungainly, heavy, a very tall, stooped man, swaying from side to side as he placed each foot down, outside edge first, staring at the sand as though he had only just learned to walk. I thought he should be ashamed to be so naked. His wrinkled wet trunks clung to his hairless legs. I put down my camera.

My little mother sat up swiftly and opened the beach bag, rooting around. A silver tube of lipstick flashed in her hand as she applied a swift dash of red to her mouth without the aid of a mirror, a specialty of hers. This was her signal that a change was imminent. She always put on lipstick when a new thing was about to happen. I started gathering my things, getting ready to go back to the rental cottage.

I glanced at my father, who was lumbering back from his walk.

That was when I saw them, down the beach by the shore: a line of Totals, tied together, led by a big woman with bright red hair. Their spade-shaped heads swayed from side to side on their slender necks like heavy buds on stems. The red-haired Englishwoman was singing "Pop Goes the Weasel," leading the Totals along the shoreline.

Half a pound of tuppenny rice,
Half a pound of treacle . . .

I wondered if one of them could be my sister. Swiftly I checked to see if my mother had noticed. She was focused on the children, her back straight in her red swimsuit. She watched as they passed in a line, hitched to one another, their frail legs marching forward. My father was now rushing toward us, his big feet dragging through the sand, alarm on his kind face.

"Candace," he said to her. "Let's go."

That night, the storm rolled off the Atlantic and rattled the glass windows of the bungalow, whipping up the trees. Lightning cracked the sky open again and again above us. Thunder boomed. My father set a cup of hot chocolate in a pool of light on the table. The outer edges of the room were in darkness. My mother had not come out of her room since we'd gotten back from the beach. Sometimes these spells lasted for weeks. I raised the cup to my lips.

"We'd better leave," he said. His bald head, like a lumpy potato, looked too big for his body.

"We have two more days." I heard the whine in my voice and was ashamed.

"There's no point, sweetheart. She'll never go back to the beach now. I'm sorry."

"Do you think E was there? On the beach?"

"Oh no, darling. She's hours away, safe in her bed."

We drove back from Montauk in the morning. When we got home, my mother slipped off the passenger seat and rushed into the house.

My mother had a hand in the early design of the Total Phone. She didn't invent it. The first set of Total Phones was cobbled together in a garage by a hairy engineer by the name of Miles Handy. But my then young mother, Candace Hardwick, was a known force among the glittering pool of genius that spawned new gadgets in those days, and she was part of the team assigned the task of making the Total Phone portable, affordable, and salable. My mother was fascinated by the idea that technology might alleviate alienation and loneliness, create positive emotion, jiggle the electrons of a person around just so to create a feeling of absolute peace and connection with other human beings, all without using drugs. In the early days of the Total Phone's development, when I was a toddler, my mother practically lived in the booth you had to strap yourself into to use the thing. She was an addict. She made a lot of Total calls to a coworker named Saul, mind-melding through the night, tears of ecstasy streaming down her face. As you can imagine, there were a lot of Total betrayals in that period. You didn't have to be in the same room or even the same country to have the most intimate and complete experience of your life. Anyway, my father was upset. It nearly ended their marriage. They stayed together because of the pregnancy. My father was a stand-up guy. When the baby was born, the small-town doctors didn't know what to say. They had never seen anything like it. It was my mother who told them that E was a Total. It was my mother who drove her, still mewing like a kitten, to the Total Care Center in Greenwich, and dropped her off without discussing it with my father. She then drove home, went to bed, and stayed there for two years.

It was the last week of summer. In a few days I would go back to boarding school. The sun flashed through the trees as we drove. I tilted my head up, shut my eyes, and saw red flares of sunlight as they passed through my eyelids, jolting me over and over.

"What are you doing?" my mother asked. "You look like you're having a fit."

"If you close your eyes, the light makes you twitch," I said.

"Yes," she said. "I remember that. I haven't done that in a lot of years. You'd think I'd have time, but it never occurs to me to shut my eyes when Dad is driving."

"Because he's such a bad driver," I said, and she smiled.

"He isn't good with the physical world."

"I need a rain jacket," I said.

"Oh, Noodle, why do you tell me everything at the last minute?"

"Mine is short in the sleeves, I just tried it on."

"I'll order one," she said.

The Total Care Center was vast, a series of flat-roofed

white structures, like an industrial park, with ambulances outside. My mother parked and turned to me. She looked embarrassed.

"Maybe you should stay in the car," she said.

"I didn't come with you to stay in the car," I said.

"Why did you?" she asked, looking straight over the steering wheel.

"I want to see her," I said.

There were a few other families in the waiting room. No one was speaking. My mother and I sat on a white vinyl couch. She sat up very straight, her small hands clamped together, her lips glistening red.

A nurse in scrubs emerged, holding a female Total by the hand. The elfin child blinked in the light, her flaxen hair wavy and fine, as if each strand had been painted with a one-haired brush, like a Renaissance angel. Her large, triangular head seemed to float atop a slender neck. She wore a simple white tunic. My mother rushed up to the child and gave her the outsize lollipop we had brought with us, a flat disk of swirling color.

I knew it wasn't E. I hadn't seen my sister in three years, since she was five, but I knew it was the wrong girl. The nurse whispered to my mother, taking the lollipop, still wrapped in cellophane, from the child's hand. The Total let her hand drop, as though accustomed to having no possessions. The nurse led her away, through another door. I looked at my mother. She had returned to the vinyl couch and was smiling, staring at the place where she had made her mistake. Now another nurse entered, holding E by the hand. She was identical to the other girl, but she was E. She looked at my mother, and her mouth opened slightly, revealing tiny porcelain china-doll teeth. Her high blue eyes widened. My mother walked over more tentatively this time, glancing at the nurse, who smiled. Then she knelt before E and gave her the lollipop. My sister took the sweet and rested its crinkly wrapping against her forehead.

I thought, I am going to get you out of here.

I began to hatch my plan as soon as I got back to boarding school. Holly Talbot and I were walking down the path from our dorm when I told her I wanted to spring E from the Center, run away, go on the lam, start my life.

"I'm sixteen, after all," I said. "I don't legally have to go to school anymore."

"What will you do for money, Roxanne?" Holly asked, squinting at me. Holly loved money and planned to make piles of it.

"I'll get jobs. I'll take her out to the West Coast."

"You could be an exotic dancer."

"I can't be a stripper; my middle is too fat."

"You're totally sexy and you don't even know it," said Holly. "Look at those lips." She took a handful of my lips and squeezed. "I would give anything for that mouth." Holly did have very thin lips.

The fall snapped into focus, a blaze of red and yellow. Then the landscape started drabbing back down again. The days at the school were short and muzzy. I was on a slow boil about my mother not having recognized E at the Total Care Center. I truly hated her for the first time in my life. I made excuses not to come home for weekends and went to Holly's parents' house in Greenwich for Thanksgiving. My mother was taken aback when I told her, but she accepted my decision with surprising speed. I sensed shame in her voice.

The Total Care Center was very close to Holly's parents' house. I discovered this as Holly's red-faced father, Mr. Talbot, drove us to their place from the school and passed it without a glance. The buildings, single-storied, immaculate, white with shiny black steel roofs, seemed to make no impression whatsoever on his satisfied mind. I imagined my sister locked in her cell on Thanksgiving Day, opening her mouth, her already wide eyes widening high up on that triangular head as she imagined her mother, who was nowhere. I would be her mother now.

Holly's parents were super gregarious but conservative. Often I wondered how they felt about having a daughter who stalked around their country house in tight leather pants and spent her nights with local boys she snuck in through the back door. I was still a virgin. Holly was a proud slut. I admired her for this.

The Talbots seemed to have retired. They spent every winter on their boat (actually a yacht the size of an ocean liner) in the Bahamas. They flew Holly out for two weeks at Christmas. The rest of the winter, while Mr. and Mrs. Talbot were basting themselves like roast turkeys on the deck of their yacht, Holly would be snorting coke and dragging boys through her window in boarding school, and the house in Greenwich would lie empty, with only the housekeeper coming in a few days a week to fluff up the pillows.

Mr. Talbot looked like he was filled to the brim with

meat. That Thanksgiving, Scotch in hand, he gave me a ro-
bust explanation of the Talbot lifestyle, punctuated by sudden, unpredictable guffaws, while his wife, a solidly built
woman with a light dusting of fair hair on her cheeks, smiled
in a knowing, wise, possibly sarcastic way.

"At a certain stage in my life, I realized I could live however I wanted," Mr. Talbot said, an amused expression on his
face. "I mean, in terms of *scheduling*." And then he exploded
in phlegmy laughter as his wife maintained her rigid smile.

That night, as we lay on Holly's twin beds, facing each
other, Holly helped me work out my plan. That weekend I
would visit my sister at the Total Care Center, alone. The Talbots' gardener, Dave, who sold Holly weed and owed her
some favors, would drive me there early in the morning, before her parents were conscious. That way the staff at the Center would remember me when I came back, and think it was
normal for my sister to walk around the grounds with me.

"My parents leave for the winter on December first. We
can come here if we get E on a weekend. But we have to be
out by Sunday night, because Mrs. Stone comes in Monday
morning, and she calls the 'rents about absolutely everything."
I knew Holly's parents had had more than one alarming call
from Mrs. Stone while they were on that yacht, though I had
not been at the house for the epic party that really sealed the
deal, when Mrs. Stone let herself in one Sunday morning,
having forgotten to close the upstairs windows, only to find a
raft of beautiful naked kids draped unconscious all over the
chintz-upholstered furniture. She started screaming, convinced she'd walked in on some sort of Manson Family situation and that they were all dead. Her hysteria revived the

teenagers and they peered at her, universally high, until one of them, the son of a prominent judge on the D.C. circuit, attempted to initiate a conversation about the weather with a pillow clamped modestly over his lap. Furious, Mrs. Stone called Holly's parents, who promptly forbade their treasured daughter to ever use the house again when they were away.

Dave the gardener drove the small truck with jerky, impatient maneuvers, as though he were pissed off at the steering wheel and gearshift. Each time he moved his skinny arms, a waft of tobacco and stale sweat emanated from his side of the car. His fingernails were rimmed with green. I wondered about the sequence of events that had led Dave to become the Talbots' gardener, and whether he and Holly had rolled around together yet. He had a grimy appeal.

"You're quiet, huh?" said Dave.

"It's just early," I said. A fringe of meager beard edged Dave's jaw and climbed up his drawn cheek.

"I'm up this early every day," he said.

"Me, too," I said. "For school."

"Were you and Holly up late?" His loose-knit brown sweater had a hole in the chest, as though someone had taken a bite out of it.

"I guess," I said.

"Holly's funny," he said.

When I walked up to the desk in the front lobby of the Total Care Center, the receptionist looked up at me curiously. Behind her, the visitors' center was hung with shiny cardboard turkeys and decorations with Native American motifs.

"Can I help you?"

"I'm Roxanne Hunt," I said. "My mother is Candace Hardwick? My sister is E . . . Eva Hunt."

"Oh, yes, of course," the woman said. "I remember you from a few months ago—I remember your red hair." I wondered if she also remembered my mother not recognizing her child. "Is that your natural color?" she asked, her pretty, plump face turned up at me.

"Uh-huh," I said. I noticed that her name tag read GERALDINE.

Geraldine peered into her computer. "I don't think we have you on the books for a visit. Is your mother parking?"

"No, I'm staying with friends for the holiday, they live nearby, and . . . my mom said it was okay if I visited E alone, because I said I wanted to spend some time with her alone. I'm hoping to . . . to come here more, on my own," I said, repeating the lines I had rehearsed with Holly.

"I'll have to call your mother," Geraldine said, looking at me carefully. "Just to confirm the visit." I watched the place where the receiver was clamped over her ear. There was a fine blue vein that traveled along her fleshy jaw, just beneath the skin.

"Hello? Hello, Ms. Hardwick? This is Geraldine from the Total Care Center, and everything is fine. I'm just calling to say we have your daughter Roxanne here; she's here to visit Eva, and we didn't have the visit on the books, so . . . we . . ."

The woman hung on the line for a long moment. I could actually feel my mother pausing, her mind racing as she tried to figure out what I was doing, what game I was playing, turning up to visit E alone in this way. I knew what she was thinking. She was thinking I had done it to show her up, to show I was a better person than she was.

Geraldine furrowed her brow. "Hello?" she said. Then a little smile spasmed the corner of her mouth as she looked at me. "Wonderful. I just had to check. Happy Thanksgiving!"

She hung up the phone.

"Did my mom forget I was coming?" I asked.

"Yes, she had to check her datebook," Geraldine said. It had taken my mother a few seconds to collect her wits, but she'd managed.

"Now, let's see." Geraldine checked her computer. "Eva should be at music time right now. I'll have her brought up."

"Could I . . . would I be allowed to take her on a little walk?" I asked. "Just, just around the building?"

"Let's see how she is with you first, okay?"

"Sure," I said.

E's hand was slack, cool. It weighed nearly nothing. I gripped it between my thumb and forefinger and led her around the sunny visitors' room, toward a table with colorful blocks stacked up on it.

She stood, serene, pale, her arrow-shaped head swaying slightly on its thin stalk of a neck. Her high blue eyes, so clear they were nearly translucent, focused on the wooden blocks. I took her meager fingers and brushed them against a block. With sudden will, she grasped it. She then put it to her forehead, as she had done with the lollipop my mother gave her.

"I'm your sister," I whispered. "I'm Roxanne."

The garden was a circle of brownish-green lawn edged with a border of neat hedge. We sat together on a bench. On the other side of the lawn, a man wearing fluffy earmuffs was doing calisthenics in front of a group of five male Totals. Each Total had a nurse behind him, who held the child's arms, imitating what the teacher was doing, lifting him off the ground when the man jumped. The Totals seemed to have no capacity to imitate the man's movement, and no interest in the exercise. I wondered how much it must cost to keep a Total in a place with so many nurses. E sat beside me, wearing an immaculate white puffy parka with white fake-fur trim on the hood. She also wore padded white pants and snow boots. Totals were very susceptible to cold. Two rosy marks had bloomed on her cheeks, and her eyes sparkled. I had taken a ball from the visitors' area and held it in front of her.

"Want to play catch?" I asked. I stood, took E under her arms, and lifted her off the bench, standing her upright, then walked a few paces away from her. I held the red ball up in the air. E followed it with her gaze. "Here," I said. "Catch." I lobbed the ball at her gently. It bounced off her stomach and rolled to the ground. She made no move to catch it. She seemed to be focused on my face. She looked like she was thinking.

I asked to see E's room. The nurse, a fair-haired man in tight green scrubs, led me down a long white hallway. Every few feet, there was an open door. The rooms were small, outfitted with complicated-looking beds that had tubes coming out of them. Some of the beds had Total children in them. They looked unwell. They lay immobile, plastic masks strapped to their faces. When we came to room 306, we stopped.

"This is Eva's room," said the nurse. I walked into what looked like the cell of an astronaut nun. Everything was white; electronic panels were set into the wall beside the narrow bed.

Not one drawer was open, not a sheet of paper lay on the table, nor a pair of shoes on the floor.

"Doesn't she have any stuffed animals?" I asked.

"Totals don't like them," said the nurse. "Freaks them out." Hot air blew out of a vent above the bed. The nurse unzipped E's parka and took off her snow pants. He folded the clothes and put them into a drawer. I took note of where E's things were kept. E stood in her white silk long underwear, completely still, seemingly inanimate. "You've tuckered her out," said the nurse.

"Is she . . . healthy?" I asked.

"Yes," he said, wiping the sweat from his forehead. "That is, as healthy as a Total gets. They're delicate. They can take a turn at any time, to be perfectly honest."

"What keeps them healthy?"

"Well, in all honesty, Totals are still a mystery," said the nurse, walking into the bathroom and turning on the bath. "They're prone to sudden illness. But it does seem like they thrive with engagement."

"Engagement?"

He popped his head out of the bathroom. E still hadn't moved. She looked like she might be listening to the soft rain falling on the metal roof.

"There was a study that indicated that Totals that aren't bored last longer," said the nurse. "That's why we have them doing activities from dawn till dusk—of course, rest is important, too."

"What about people? Contact with people, with families?"

"We don't know much about family contact here. But the staff-to-Total ratio is one to three, so they have plenty of contact. To be honest, honey, I don't think they notice who it is." I looked at the man, with his sweaty face, and wondered if he could be trusted with my sister.

I went home for Christmas. Holly flew to the Bahamas. At home, it was the usual round of parties—people singing around a piano, drunken entrepreneurs and IT people conversing in large New England farmhouses, their children, often high on their parents' prescription drugs, smiling idiotically through torturous dinners. The only kid I liked in that bunch was named Jack. He was a violinist. He had eyes that dipped down a little on the outer corners and very long, straight lashes. He was husky and sweet, handsome and kind. If I hadn't been so obsessed with kidnapping my sister at that moment in my life, I might have tried to flirt with him. Instead, I talked to him about E.

"I only know one other family with a Total," Jack said. "But it died in a week."

"Were they relieved?"

"I don't know," he said. "They're my parents' friends. My mother never had the phone, because my dad said we couldn't afford one. Now she's grateful."

"My mom helped invent them," I said. "And now she can hardly look at my sister."

"Man is a frightening animal," said Jack, plucking a mini lobster roll off a passing tray and popping it into his mouth.

"Are you good at keeping secrets?" I said.

"No," said Jack.

I was quiet then. "That is," he said, "yes, but don't tell me. You don't know me well enough to tell me a secret."

"I've known you since I was five," I said.

"You see me once a year at one of the Christmas freak shows," he said. "We don't know each other at all, Roxanne."

It had snowed heavily the night before, maybe six inches, and a sugary crust had formed on the snow. As Holly and I walked, our boots made a little *pock* sound every time we broke through, into the soft powder. Dave the gardener had driven us part of the way, then we'd gotten out and walked to the Center. Holly's parents were on the boat for the winter; her house was empty. We had spent the night alone, watching old shows and eating defrosted pizzas. Dave had stopped in to drop off a package wrapped in wax paper and cellophane, which Holly put away in her backpack.

The plan was that I would visit E, as I had many times now. Each time, I had led her outside and taken her picture, so there would be nothing out of the ordinary in that.

I introduced Holly to Geraldine at the desk, and Geraldine didn't even think of calling my mother to check if an extra visitor was approved. She was now so used to me coming to see my sister, she barely looked up when I arrived, just pointed her soft doll's face in my direction and winked.

E was already waiting in the visitors' area, standing beside Charlie, the weekend nurse with the tight scrubs.

"There she is!" he exclaimed as I walked in. Holly walked over to E, folding her svelte frame in half, putting her palms on her knees and staring.

"Wow," she whispered.

E looked back at her, her head wavering slightly.

"She's looking at me," Holly said.

"She's looking at you 'cause you're looking at her," I said.

Out in the yard, I took a photograph of E with my camera as she sat on the bench, her little hands in their white mittens resting in her lap, her gaze somewhere in the distance. Holly stood behind me.

"She's like a fairy creature," Holly said. "Like something out of a book."

Holly and I walked E around the perimeter of the garden. I was holding one of her slight, mittened hands; Holly held the other. E was not heavy enough to break the surface of the snow, so she walked on the sugary crust. She was so light, as light as a small dog, I thought.

It was a gray morning. The Center glowed with incandescent light. The many solar panels on the roof gleamed like facets of a fly's eye. There were no other Totals or nurses outside. No one seemed to be watching. There were cameras, of course, all over the building, but by the time they watched the footage of us stealing E, we would be on our way to California.

I picked E up and carried her once we were a few feet into the woods. Her little body felt stiff. I could hear her breathing in my ear.

"We're going someplace warm," I said.

The bare trees arched over our heads. We hurried through the woods, our feet cracking branches and stepping over roots. NO TRESPASSING signs had been put up at regular intervals, stapled into the trees around the Center. As we tramped through the snow, Holly's phone pronounced directions to us in a male English accent, a voice she had chosen because she loved pretending she had an English butler.

"Please turn right," the suave voice entreated.

"Thank you, Jeeves," Holly said, her pointy face screwed up against the cold.

"My pleasure," answered the voice.

After a few minutes, I stopped, put E down, and took an energy drink from my backpack. In my reading about Totals, I had learned that they could never be allowed to get dehydrated. They needed a regular infusion of fluids. I popped the beveled straw though the thin plastic hymen protecting the opening of the drink pouch and handed it to E. She didn't react. I put the straw to her mouth. Her tiny pink tongue reached out to the straw and guided it between her porcelain doll's teeth, then her lips pursed around the straw and she sucked lustily, her eyes unfocused, as I held the packet.

"She was thirsty," said Holly, shoulders hunched in her thin pink jacket. She was, as usual, underdressed.

Once E had sucked the pouch dry, I picked her up again, and we kept walking, following Jeeves's plummy voice through the snow. "Please continue in a northeasterly direction," the voice said.

"I imagine him as being tall, but stooped," Holly said, cradling her phone to her chest. "He's got big hands, perfect nails. He's bald."

"Bald?"

"Not completely bald. You want me to take her?"

"I'm fine," I said.

". . . he's got hair around the sides of his head, but what he does have is an amazing body. And at night when he's off duty, he takes off his butler uniform and he's totally into me."

"Holly," I said. "I'm not judging your butler fantasy. But I'm starting to wonder if he's getting us lost."

After an extra half hour of turning in circles, we reached the road. There was Dave, his exhausted face behind the dirty window of the idling truck. I got in the back with E and put on her safety belt. It was then that I saw one side of her lower lip tugged down, as though by a string, exposing her teeth. "Look," I said. "I think she's smiling."

Holly swiveled around in her seat to see. From E's glassy eye, a tear trickled down the long, flat expanse of her face.

"Oh, God," said Holly. "Maybe she's scared." I moved close to E and tried to hug her, but her slight body remained limp in the seat. I dried her tear and kissed her.

"Don't worry," I whispered. "I'm going to take care of you."

My plan for E's abduction shone with Holly's genius and reflected the many nights we'd spent planning in her twin beds while Mr. Talbot drank Scotch and sodas downstairs, adding new veins to the squiggling masses already decorating his nose, and his wife sat in sardonic silence, her fuzzy face set in that strange and furious smile. We could not take a plane or a train, because the police would be looking for us. Neither of us had a driver's license, even for self-driving cars, and Dave was willing to chauffeur us for this one morning only. But Holly knew a band that was going on tour and would give us a ride. So we had Dave drive us to Hartford, where there was an enormous bus in a parking lot, and waited there for the band to arrive. E was sleeping, slumped in her seat. I was worried we had tired her out too much.

After a while, a slender, dark-skinned man in a navy blue uniform slinked out of the bus. He opened the luggage bin and started sorting out some crates in there. Holly got out of the truck and waved.

"Excuse me!" Bent double in the luggage hold, the man began to turn.

"I'm a friend of the band's. Of Dougie's. My name is Holly Talbot."

"I am Manfred Young," said the man, in an elegant accent.

"Dougie said he told you about us, maybe we could wait in the bus?"

Manfred, crouched, looked out at Holly with catlike calm.

We climbed onto the bus. I gave E exactly the portion of mushed-up meat and vegetables Charlie the nurse fed her every night, from one of the crate's worth of Total Meals I had stolen, a few at a time, from the Center over the previous months. She ate her food with expressionless, rote movements, opening her mouth like a baby bird after each bite. It smelled like gravy. Afterward I took her to the bathroom, put her in her pajamas, brushed her teeth carefully, and lifted her into one of the bunks toward the back, snuggling in beside her. I clicked in the protective netting that would prevent us from flying around the bus if there were any sudden turns.

Once E was lying down, her eyes closed automatically, like a doll's. A few minutes later, the band clattered in. I watched them through the netting as Holly, who had changed into her leather pants and a tight white tank top, greeted them all with the swagger of a western madam. They were three boys and one Asian girl with a shaved and bleached blond head, her long, strong arms emerging from a leather vest. I gathered her name was Joy. She looked around the bus with wonder.

"Oh, man, this is the shit," Joy said to Holly. "We've been living in a van for four years."

"I rented it so we could all lie down," said Holly, who was brushing her hair.

I couldn't make out the boys too well from my perch. One of them had wild, tangled hair. Another had a beard. The third seemed younger than the rest. He had a normal haircut, wore regular clothes, and sat in the back of the bus, away from the others. I could hear Holly explaining about E. They all looked up at our bunk, but I stayed immobile. E was asleep beside me. As the self-driving bus started moving, monitored watchfully by Manfred, Holly took the package of drugs out of her backpack and handed it to Joy, who unwrapped it carefully. Soon Holly and her new friends were all hunched over lines of white powder. The boy who had sequestered himself in the back of the bus went into the restroom, came out, then stripped down to his underwear and climbed into his bunk, which was opposite mine. As he clicked the netting in over himself, he looked over and caught me staring.

"Hi," he said. "I'm Harvest."

"I'm Roxanne," I said. Then I turned away from him,

toward E, who was lying on her back. I snuggled into her body. She felt so warm.

It took us three days to get to Los Angeles. I took impeccable care of E. I hydrated her regularly and gave her all her meals. I washed her as best I could in the tiny shower they had on the bus. I took her for walks whenever we were sure no one would see her. A stray Total was a newsworthy event—especially a Total on tour with a futuretech band. Each moment I had with her I tried to make special. I wanted her to feel loved. In truth, I had no idea what E was feeling. Since the moment her tear fell when I thought she was smiling, she had betrayed no emotion. Her arrow-shaped head with its pointed chin, her lovely, high blue eyes, her tiny nose and mouth, those little teeth—they remained an inscrutable mask. I kept taking pictures of E, but also of the band. My best pictures were of Harvest. His eyes were moist and sort of pleading. I began to understand that he was in love with the girl singer, Joy. He loved her in a hapless way because she was with Troy, the boy with the beard. Joy and Troy. So poor, normal-looking Harvest would sit in the gloomy back of the bus, fingering his guitar and playing sad songs in a minor key, as the others snorted coke and fucked and had a hearty time. Meanwhile, I mothered E and began to moon over Harvest.

Holly read about our disappearance on the internet and was thrilled by the attention, though she was disgusted by the school photo of her that her parents had given the press, in which she was wearing a kilt and a tortoiseshell headband, her gorgeous breasts hidden in the folds of her Fair Isle sweater. Given the fact that we were now known fugitives, we decided to try living in a motel on the outskirts of L.A., a place the band knew. They said it was cheap but had a nice pool and clean rooms and was close to a little mall with restaurants and a grocery store. Holly's plan was to work as a stripper for a while, even though she had a trust fund and had taken a vast amount of cash from various automated teller machines in preparation for our trip. She knew she'd be expelled from boarding school for this escapade, so she planned to take the year, strip, maybe get into some crime, then graduate from some other boarding school, go to Smith or Dartmouth, her parents' alma maters, and then law school. Her idea was to have a really fascinating story and then get a book deal so that she could be rich before she even became a lawyer. As it turned out, all of this came to pass for Holly.

On the bus, Holly spent half her days asleep beside Dougie, the sound engineer with the matted hair. Dougie had a fish scale body tattoo covering his arms and legs and a beer belly. Holly had become the bank for the group, buying us dinner whenever we stopped. I felt embarrassed by all this extravagance and felt that I should pay my share, but I didn't have the resources Holly did, and she seemed to be absolutely loaded. She paid for everything with cash so that no one could trace her through any bank transactions. We had shut down our phones. No one had any idea where we were. Holly was a born criminal.

The Motel Iguana was situated on a stretch of desert highway. It was dawn when we arrived. A delicate pink sky silhouetted the cratered landscape. The band had been here many times, apparently, and greeted the undead-looking night clerk—a stiff, pasty, sour-looking man—as if he were a favorite uncle.

E and I had a room to ourselves. Our window looked out onto the pool. Once night fell, the pool lights came on and the rectangle of blue light hovered in the blackness. The night sky was festooned with webs of stars so bright they looked fake. Occasionally a pair of headlights appeared far off and wound their way to us, then, inevitably, passed. I stood at the window looking out at this spectacle for a long while after I had put E to bed in a clean pair of pajamas. I turned to check on her and there she was, sitting up in the double bed, staring past me out the window.

"It's cool, huh?" I asked her. I wondered if maybe she was still asleep, because her eyes were unblinking and her head was wavering a little, as if it were heavy. I was about to walk over to her and tuck her back in when she opened her mouth really wide. At first I thought she was yawning. I had never seen her yawn. But then this terrible sound started coming out of her mouth. It was a bellowing scream. It just kept coming and coming. She was staring out that window, screaming at something. Her white teeth shone inside her open mouth, her tiny body rigid, her hands like claws. She terrified me. My heart rocked my chest. I didn't dare touch her while she was like that. Someone knocked on the door.

"Who is it?" I yelled.

"It's Harvest." I opened the door. E went silent and turned at the noise, watching him as he came into the room. Her chest was still heaving from the screams.

"What happened?" he asked.

"I don't know," I said. "We were just looking out the

window." I felt braver now that Harvest was in the room. I walked up to E and stroked her head. Her breath came in little shudders. I gave her some water out of her sippy cup. She took a couple of gulps and lay down.

"Don't worry," I whispered, "you're fine." She looked up at me then, and her recognition came like a shock. And not just recognition. Trust. Then she shut her eyes and seemed to sleep.

I asked Harvest if he would stay for a while to be sure E was okay. He sat in the chair by the window, his form etched by the light from the pool and maybe the stars. The rectangle of the pool pushed itself into space within the window frame behind him. We talked for hours. Harvest told me how he and Joy had started the band when they were still in high school, how they had been a couple then, how she was the first girl he'd ever slept with. He described how brave Joy was, how talented, and how much she had changed in the past couple of years, since the band had started getting successful. He talked about the town they grew up in, Nebraska City, Nebraska. Joy had moved there when she was seven. She was the only Asian kid in the school. Nebraska City was on the Missouri River. In winter they sometimes skated on the river, holding hands. Harvest talked about his parents, who were both anesthesiologists. He had a sister named Pam. Harvest looked over at me occasionally as he talked, and I wondered what he saw. I had a view of myself in the mirror opposite the bed. My auburn hair was down to my waist. I was wearing a T-shirt and jeans. I thought my face looked pretty. I wished I was closer to Harvest, but I couldn't figure out how to get over to his chair. Finally the dawn came. I walked over to the window and looked out at the sunrise, lifting my heavy hair off my neck and arching my back in what I hoped was an alluring pose. Harvest was looking at E.

"Why did you take her out of that place?" he asked.

"I want her to have a real life before she dies," I said. "And they say Totals live longer when they're loved."

"But how do you know what *she* wants?" Harvest asked me, looking up at me with an unpleasant, accusatory expression.

"She's my sister and I've learned how to take care of her," I said, and as I said it, I immediately realized that he was right, that I had no idea what she wanted.

"Seems like this trip is more about you than about her," he said, and got up. "I'll see you," he said, and clicked the door shut behind him.

I walked over to E. She was flat on her back, eyes shut tight. I took off my pants and got into bed beside her, cuddled into her. I could feel warm tears of shame flowing along the bridge of my nose until I fell asleep.

Later that morning, when I was brushing E's teeth, one of her molars popped off as if it had been adhered with rubber cement. I reached into her wet mouth and took out the tooth. It had no roots. When E spat out her toothpaste, there was blood mixed with her saliva. I remembered that Totals had only one set of teeth. This was the beginning of the end. I looked at my sister, who was playing with the hotel soap, letting it slip around between her bony fingers.

Holly and the band were all still sleeping. I walked E along the highway to the Dollar Store in the strip mall. I had not yet taken her out in public, but this area seemed so isolated from the rest of the world, so beyond the realm of The News, I couldn't imagine it would be a problem. Or maybe by then I had started to wish I would be caught. Anyway, we walked about five minutes in the blazing heat to the Dollar Store. I shielded E from the heat with a black umbrella I had packed just in case. It was my mother's. A minivan passed and a whole family of people turned their heads to stare at us.

Inside, the Dollar Store was too cool, almost frigid. I immediately became frightened that E would catch cold. I pulled a terry-cloth robe from a rack and pulled it over her. A scrawny woman who was pricing mugs saw this.

"I just don't want her to get cold," I said. She stared at E. Maybe she didn't know about Totals. She certainly had never been the owner of a Total Phone.

"Sure, honey," the woman said. "God bless."

The pool was tepid. E stood with her stick arms pushed out by the rubber rings around her biceps. The bathing suit I had bought at the Dollar Store was sky blue, with a little frill and a picture of a big-eyed mermaid drawn in sequins on the tummy. E was covered in a whitish layer of sunscreen and wore a terry-cloth hat. I had bought an extra-large hat, and even that barely fit over the corners of her skull. Still, I thought she looked cute like that. I led her to the edge of the pool and walked into the water while still holding her hand.

"It's kind of like a bath," I said. E stared at the glimmering water, transfixed. I took her under the arms and held her over the water. She pulled her feet up, not wanting to get wet. Still,

I dipped her toes into the pool, then raised her up high. A sound came out of her that sounded like a chirp. I did it again, skimming her feet along the surface of the water, then lifting her up. She chirped again. By now I had become wary of E's emotional signals. I was ready for her to start screaming. But each time I dipped her into the pool, the little chirp flew out of her. Gradually I realized that she was laughing. I dipped her a little farther in each time, until she was really getting wet, and the chirps became shrieks of delight. After a long while of plunging her in and raising her up again, my arms got tired, so I just cradled her like a bride and whooshed her around in the water. She let her body relax and set her head in the crook of my arm. She looked up at the sky. Her blue eyes were tranquil. She looked happy.

Later, when E was napping in her robe on a lawn chair, shaded by my mother's black umbrella, which I had leaned on the side of her chaise, and I was drying myself by the side of the pool in my one-piece, I noticed Manfred, the driver, on a patch of grass behind the motel, performing karate moves in a yellow sun visor and a brown Speedo that blended in with his skin so well that at first glance I thought he was naked. Manfred kicked out fast, his lean muscles rippling.

Eventually, the band and Holly straggled out of their rooms. Holly was in a bikini, her long, lean legs and concave tummy on full display. I looked down at my little roll of pudge and covered myself with a towel. Joy and Troy emerged from their room in T-shirts and underwear. Joy was drinking a Coke and wore a huge pair of sunglasses. Her shaved blond head set off her tawny skin. She wore a big silver ring on the middle finger of her left hand.

"How's it going, Rox?" she asked me.

"Okay," I said, embarrassed and pleased that Joy had spoken to me and given me a nickname, all in one go. She looked over at E.

"She good?"

"I think so. She really had fun in the pool."

"We were watching you," said Joy, jutting her head in the direction of her window. "You're a really nice person." Just then, Harvest emerged. I hoped he'd heard. He sat down a few feet apart from the others and put his feet in the water morosely.

"Hey, Harvest Moon," said Joy, walking over to him and putting her arm around him in a sisterly way. "We got a gig tonight."

"I'm aware of that," said Harvest.

"I'm just trying to boost morale," said Joy, walking back over to Troy and taking a cigarette from a pack in his T-shirt pocket. "Fuck."

"What time are we going to be in L.A.?" Holly asked, slathering suntan oil over her legs.

"Sound check's at six," said Dougie. "We should take a powder by three."

"Take a powder?" asked Holly, surprised.

"It just means leave," said Dougie. "Although we could also take some powder," he added, kissing Holly sloppily. She pushed him away as if he were a slobbering dog.

"Not before the gig," said Harvest.

"No, only cocoa before the gig," said Joy mockingly, ripping off her T-shirt and revealing her naked chest. She had very dark nipples. Harvest looked like he was about to cry.

"I have no wish to get arrested," said Manfred, who had finished his karate and was entering the pool gingerly, still in his yellow visor, his arms held above the water as though it were freezing.

"Why would you get arrested?" asked Joy. "I'm the one who's naked."

"Well may you ask," said Manfred, plunging into a choppy breaststroke. Holly narrowed her eyes, watching him. I knew that look well.

"Where do you live, Manfred?" she asked.

"In Hollywood," said Manfred in his clipped, foreign English. "In the heart of the matter."

"And what do you do when you're not, like, monitoring a bus or acting like Bruce Lee?"

"I write."

"Screenplays?"

"I am an essayist," said Manfred, turning and swimming the other way.

"How come you ended up in L.A.?"

"My subject is the decline of civilization," he said, craning his neck so his hair wouldn't get wet. "Also, I love the weather, and I was left a house."

I had thought a few times about calling my mother and letting her know where we were. I couldn't shake a sense of wrong-doing. Once we'd eased into Los Angeles in our enormous vehicle, Manfred sitting vigilantly as always as the wheel turned of its own accord, we stopped at a gas station, where I bought a disposable phone. Manfred leaned against a wall nearby, drinking a bottle of green juice with a paper straw, as I punched out my parents' number. My eyes were on the bus, where E was sleeping. Holly was watching over her.

My mother answered after the first ring.

"Hello?" Her voice sounded anxious, speedy.

"Hi, Mom."

A long silence followed. My father came to the phone.

"Roxanne. Sweetheart, where are you?"

"I just wanted you guys to know that we're safe."

"Please come home now. Mommy is very upset."

"Is she?"

"Of course she is."

"Why?"

"Because she loves you so much."

I could see them sitting in the kitchen, his worried potato head and her frantic little body huddled around the phone. She was listening in. I could hear her breathing. Even her silence was a ploy. I hung up and threw the phone away.

Manfred stepped out from the shadow of the building.

"You know, Roxanne, you should bring that little creature back to her mother," he said, looking down at me. His yellow visor cast a jaundiced glow on his blue-black skin, making him look green.

"Were you listening to my conversation?" I asked.

"I don't have to. I can imagine your story. I am a writer, after all," he added, smiling to reveal his strong, white, prominent canines. His eyes were black, the whites gleaming. Manfred was the healthiest-looking person I had ever seen.

As I climbed the steps onto the bus, I met Harvest descending. He looked disheveled and had clearly just woken up. As he passed me, he touched my fingers, sort of half held my hand, then let go. I looked up at him, confused. I had thought he despised me. He didn't return my glance, just walked off the bus as the doors closed with a hiss.

In the back, Holly was reading on a tablet.

"She's still sleeping, I just checked her," she said.

"I talked to my mom," I said.

"What did you do that for?"

"I used a burner phone. I just wanted her to know we were okay."

"What did she say?" asked Holly, squinting up at me peevishly from the tablet. Her glamour was in her body, I realized, in the way she moved and spoke. When she was just sitting there, in a sweatshirt, she looked like a skinny kid.

"She asked where we were," I said.

"The sooner we all split up, the less likely they are to find us," she said.

"What do you mean?"

"I mean they know you and I are together and, who knows, they might have figured out about the band. I say we go to the concert tonight and then go our separate ways."

I thought about this and began to panic.

"Where will you go?"

"Manfred said I could stay with him for a while. I've fallen for him big time."

"When did you have time to fall for Manfred?"

"Remember that little gap between when he went swimming and when we all got on the bus?"

"Yeah."

"Then."

"Wow."

"You wanted to start a new life," Holly said, waving her hand.

Harvest got back on the bus just then. He sat down near the front and turned toward me.

"Hey, Rox," he said.

I walked over to him, my palms skimming the rough tops of the seats. "What?" I asked. Harvest patted the seat beside him. I sat down, feeling the warmth of his body on my arm. He opened a paper bag. It was full of candy.

"I wasn't sure what you liked," he said. I looked through the selection and took out a Snickers bar.

"A classic," he said. This was the most he had said to me since the night he'd talked about himself until dawn and then insulted me. I wanted to ask him why he suddenly seemed to like me, but my shyness made me mute. I figured it had something to do with Joy. And, yes, when she walked onto the bus with Troy trailing behind her, her eyes fell on the two of us in a way that made it seem she wasn't so happy. Manfred got back on, slender in his navy blue uniform, peering along the seats, counting his passengers. Dougie was sulking in the back. He'd been in a foul mood ever since Holly quietly moved on to Manfred.

"The little angel is sleeping?" asked Manfred. I nodded. "Better check her," he said. Suddenly alarmed, I got up and walked over to E's berth, climbed up, and looked at her. She was on her back, eyes closed, her breaths coming slow and regular.

"She's asleep," I said. Then I walked all the way back down the bus and sat next to Harvest again. He shifted in his seat, balling up his sweatshirt to use as a pillow and resting it against the window. As he did so, his thigh pressed against mine and he left it there. I didn't move. I just felt the pressure of his leg against my own and watched the junked-up landscape flying by through the tinted windows. My heart beat hard and fast. After about an hour, I got up and checked E again. She was awake. I took her down from the bunk, brought her to the bathroom, and spoon-fed her lunch. She ate in her automatic, baby-bird fashion, opening her mouth directly after each mushy spoonful. I still had about twenty pouches of her food left. I would order more online once I had an address. When E had finished eating, I zipped up her sweater against the cool of the air-conditioning and buckled up her safety belt, my eyes trained on the back of Harvest's head. He had woken up and was sitting alone in the front. Now Joy walked over to him and stood there, lurching with the movement of the bus, her legs spread wide. Harvest said something and she laughed. Joy was dressed entirely in fluorescent orange. Orange sweatshirt, orange sweatpants. Her brown face was a perfect oval inside the hoodie. She had a slouchy, predatory way of standing. I could never, ever be sexy like that, I thought. Never in my life.

Manfred parked in front of the venue, a place called the Zipper Lounge. I stayed behind with E as the band and Dougie trudged off, carrying their instruments. The plan was to unpack at the motel once they were done with sound check and then have dinner. Junkyard Palace went on at eight. They were opening for a band called Milk, whose songs I happened to love. I looked down through the window as the famous members of Milk emerged from an enormous bus. A girl with lank brown hair got out, followed by three tattooed women and a man with an Afro. None of them carried anything. A handful of roadies in black T-shirts with MILK printed on the back lugged instruments out from the bowels of the bus and, antlike, entered the venue in a line. I followed the lead singer with my eyes. She and the man with the Afro were in the news frequently. They were unrepentant junkies, even claiming that heroin, when managed properly and combined with a raw diet and exercise, actually slowed down the aging process. It was true they both looked amazing.

Over the past few days, having E out in public had become normal, and I wasn't so careful anymore. That evening, E and I ate at a diner with the band. Manfred had taken Holly to a vegetarian restaurant. I found this funny, as Holly ate nothing but meat. E had her mush. The band ate burgers. I had tomato soup and a grilled cheese sandwich.

Harvest was sitting opposite me. "You coming to the show?" he asked.

"I guess not," I said, spooning a teaspoon of green mush into E's mouth.

"Can't we put her to bed backstage?" asked Joy, surprising me with the word "we." "It's not fair you never get to do anything."

"There's a greenroom," said Harvest. "It has a couch."

"You can watch from backstage," said Joy. She looked at me with affection. I felt a sudden sense of belonging with these people. I wished we could stay together forever, as a family.

After we got back to the motel from the diner, I dressed E in her pajamas and went to the bathroom to put on makeup. I put on glittery eye shadow, blush, and gold lip gloss. I brushed my long hair until it gleamed like burnished wood. I washed my underarms, put on deodorant, then changed into a black jumpsuit. My old leather jacket, which my mother had bought me at a flea market in Paris when she was on a business trip, shone in the white light of the bathroom. I looked at my face in the mirror for a long while. My big mouth gleamed, and my dark eyes, caked in makeup, looked like holes in my face. I felt a power rise up in me.

I heard E cough from inside the room. She was lying on the bed, looking up at the ceiling fan as it turned lazily round and round. I walked up to her and felt her forehead. If she was sick, I would have to stay in the motel. I would miss the show. Her forehead felt fine. I put her sweater on her and packed her sleeping bag into my backpack. I didn't brush her teeth. I was afraid another tooth would fall out. I carried her onto the bus.

The greenroom was small, with an old leatherette couch and yellowing walls. The carpet was stained. There was a coffee machine in the corner, a refrigerator, and several shiny brown beanbags. I set up E's bed on the couch and put her in the sleeping bag, a motel pillow under her head. As always, her eyes shut as soon as she was tucked in. I added another blanket on top of the sleeping bag, because the room was cool and I had brought one along. She looked cozy, her angelic, fine blond hair fanned out around her triangular head, the little mouth pursed, eyes shut tight. Her tiny hands rested on top of her chest.

"You look so sexy," Joy said as she busted into the room after sound check. She herself was wearing a pair of tight white pants and a silver chain-mail top that hung loose over her narrow frame and gave tantalizing glimpses of her breasts from the side. Troy came in next, plopping onto a beanbag and staring into space. Holly and Manfred were in the audience, I knew. I wondered where Harvest was.

He walked in after a few minutes and sank into a beanbag, playing his guitar very softly.

"Is this too loud?" he whispered, glancing at E.

"I don't think so. She's really asleep," I said. As he played, he looked over at Joy, who was hopping around the room listening to a huge pair of headphones, a can of Coke in her hand.

Dougie stuck his head in the room.

"Five minutes," he said.

When the time came, Joy, Troy, and Harvest walked onto the stage. The floor was packed with people there to see Milk. Harvest had strapped on a bass guitar. Troy was at the drums. Joy, gleaming in her chain mail, had an orange electric guitar hanging off her shoulders as she strode up to the mic.

"Hey, we're Junkyard Palace," she said in a low voice as she bent her shorn blond head over her guitar. And so it began. Even though there were only three of them, with Dougie in the wings working the amps and sound effects, somehow it sounded like there were ten musicians onstage, building up a relentless, despairing drone. Joy's voice, when she sang, was a howl, a yelp, a lament. I could see the audience from where I stood in the wings. People were crying, keening, going into trances. I watched Harvest, who stood immobile, a part of the unit that was the band, which had become one person. His fingers seemed to be playing a simple phrase, yet the sound coming out of his bass was immense.

When the song ended, I ran back to the greenroom to check on E. She hadn't moved.

The second song was a dance number. The audience was whirling and hopping. Then came a song filled with violence. Joy screamed. She showed her teeth. She was frightening. Then Harvest sang a song so tender it was painful. It was a song about two kids skating on a river in Nebraska. About loss. I knew this was their song—Joy and Harvest's. His voice had a high, sad, nasal twang.

I went back to the greenroom. E hadn't moved. The truth was, once I put her to bed, E always slept exactly eight hours. She never moved or woke up in the night. Then, eight hours from when she had shut her eyes, she would open them, like a good machine.

The band all walked in and took beers from the fridge. Harvest held one out to me. I took a sip. The lead singer from Milk put her head in the door, her sharp cheekbones casting shadows, her glossy dark hair throwing off light.

"Guys, that was fucking amazing," she said with a cheer-leader's smile. I suspected that she was not in fact a heroin addict.

"I want to watch you from the pit," said Joy.

"Sure," she said. "We have a bunch of wristbands."

Joy and Troy and Dougie made for the door. "You coming?" Joy asked Harvest.

Harvest shook his head. They all left.

Harvest looked over at me. He had a generous, open face, with curving lips, big eyes, and thick, floppy hair. His expression was opaque. I looked back at him, wondering what he was thinking. He held out his hand. I reached out and touched his fingers. He tugged at my hand and I lifted myself off the couch and kneeled at the floor before his beanbag. He leaned over and kissed me. His mouth felt very warm, almost hot. We kissed for a while. He held one of my breasts in his hand and a little moan escaped from him. I liked being the cause of that moan.

I looked over at E. Harvest stood, took my hand, and led me through a low doorway I had not noticed before.

We walked along a dark, narrow passageway until we came to a kind of loft space with a view of the stage. Harvest sat down, and I sat beside him on the rough boards. We were hidden in the shadows. The lead singer of Milk was singing one of my favorite songs of theirs. From our perch we could see the audience. Joy was easy to find in the crowd. She was near the front, gleaming in her chain mail, dancing furiously while Troy and Dougie looked on in professional silence, their hands in their pockets. I felt Harvest's hand on the back of my head. He lay back on his elbows. I understood what was required. I unzipped Harvest's fly and fellated him, hunched over him, while he watched Joy dance. Somehow I managed to hold on to a scrap of happiness as this was happening, but afterward I could not. The rift between us was complete. Harvest was silent, a shadow. I got up and walked back down the passageway to the greenroom.

E was not on the couch.

I looked around the room, expecting her to be standing there as she sometimes did, just staring. I went into the bathroom. She wasn't there. I looked up wildly at Harvest as he entered.

"I know this place really well," he said. "We'll find her."

We went to the ticket office and asked if they had seen a Total. We went to the merchandise stall, where they were selling pictures of Joy, with her shaved blond head, wearing a pair of aviator glasses. No one had seen E. We went to the public restrooms and looked in every stall.

"Maybe she went into the audience," Harvest said.

I walked up to the security guard, who was on his phone. "I've lost my sister," I said. "She's a Total—she's eight years old. Can you help us look for her?"

We walked through the heavy house doors. The three of us spread out and started searching. Switching on the flash-light app on my phone, I shone it near the floor. The music was so loud, it made my breastbone vibrate. E would be terri-fied in here. I started on the outside perimeter and walked all the way around the audience. When I got to the front, Joy looked at me.

"I can't find E," I shouted. Immediately Joy and Troy and Dougie started looking as well. Tears and snot were running down my face by now. I had a feeling that my innards were descending in an elevator within me, just going straight down.

After Milk finished their set and the crowd dispersed, we called the police. Two hours had elapsed and still we hadn't found E. The owner of the club came in. He was a small man with a sleep-creased face. He listened to what had happened and thought for a while, looking at the ground. Then he looked up. "Has anyone checked the basement?"

The door to the basement was open, and the stairs were sandy with dust. A network of large pipes covered in silver duct tape were fastened to the low ceiling, so we had to stoop in order to walk. It was hot down here. There were twelve people looking for E at this point: two cops, the members of Milk, the members of our band, Dougie, Holly, Manfred, the owner of the club, and me. The beams from our cell phones and the cops' flashlights crossed one another constantly. Speakers and amplifiers were stored in metal cages pushed to the edges of the room. We started moving the cages, which were on rollers, to see behind them. She might be hiding, I thought. If she had wandered out of the greenroom, she would have heard the loud music, and it might have scared her. She might be hiding somewhere. That had to be it.

"E!" I kept calling. "Come out! Come on, E, it's okay!"

The two cops had stopped moving stuff around, had their flashlights trained in the same place. They were quiet. I saw Holly's face. Her hand was over her mouth.

I walked toward the cops. One of them held his hand out to stop me. I clutched his arm, looked past him, and saw her. Her eyes were open. Her hands were clasped over her chest, as they always were when she was asleep. One of her little socks had come off, and her slender, white foot lay splayed out. On one toe, there was a bloody cut. She was lying on top of a speaker, beneath a water pipe. She had crawled in there and died like a rat.

I answered the knock on the motel room door without asking who it was. My mother walked in and opened her arms. I let her hold me.

"It wasn't your fault," she said.

We sat on the bed together. Across from us was a mirror. I looked over. It was me and my mother, sitting on the bed, holding hands, twinned. Her lips were brilliant red. I turned to double-check this. Yes, the lipstick was fresh, glistening. Her lips parted, and I saw her white teeth. I saw her sludge-green eyes, large and glassy. She took my face between her small hands, drew my head down, and kissed me on the fore-head, sealing the loop of our complicity. She had deployed me; I had released her. As I drew my head away, repulsed, I felt an ache where her lips had been. I walked into the bath-room and looked in the mirror. My mother's kiss had left a tattoo of scarlet lips in the middle of my forehead. I took a washcloth and wet it, then rubbed at the mark. The lipstick came off, but the kiss remained, crawling on my skin.

Years later, living in a house on a canal in a foreign city, I became pregnant.

I was plagued with dreams of giving birth to a Total, even though I knew that was impossible; I had never used a Total Phone and they had been banned for years. My fear got so bad that I had to see a specialist every day after work. He helped me meditate on the image of a healthy child.

Each day, I would leave his office and walk along the canal back to my home. I would buy an apple and chomp into it as I walked. Despite the hour spent in the specialist's office, con-juring up images of chubby knees and fragrant hair, I would gratify my self-hatred by imagining a baby who was mon-strous, with a ballooning head. Monstrous, or dead, rotted already, swimming in its own rot.

But when I gave birth, she was perfect.

I named her Hedda. Every hour, I nursed her and she

stared at me, locking me into her gaze. Her eyes were nearly violet. The feeling I had when she sucked the milk from my breast was druglike, stupefying. Her breath came in regular, churning rounds as she suckled. How I loved these animal encounters. They were the one respite from my memories.

One day, Hedda stood by herself and walked for the first time. She weaved away from me and turned. Something about the way she raised her slender hand for balance, the quiet, listening gaze, made me stand, not wanting to believe it. I approached her. She stood stock-still, so separate, swaying slightly with the effort of standing up. She had an elfin frame. I came close to her and knelt before her, feeling her milky breath on my face. I bowed to her mystery. What was awaiting me inside that child was unknown to me then, but I was no longer my own. I belonged to her.

SHE CAME TO ME

Driving up the helix-shaped parking garage, Ciaran Fox crept through floor after darkened floor, searching for a vacancy. Looking for a parking space in a jammed lot was just like trying to come up with a new idea for a novel, he thought as he turned the taut, leather steering wheel of his Mercedes gently, rounding the concrete curve and accelerating up yet another ramp: every time you thought you might have found one, it turned out to be taken by someone else. Sweet Jesus, why was it so fucking hard to find a space to wedge his goddamn, shitting car into? Seven floors of gleaming steel, SUVs parked hip to hip like cows eating out of their troughs. It was the women, he thought, clotting up the place with their absurdly unnecessary off-road vehicles. Did any of them actually need to drive today? Carbon footprints as big as bathtubs, and for what? To shop, in all probability.

Ciaran emerged at the vivid sky. The final floor. And there it was. His space. A nasty, inconvenient little gap between two gleaming monsters. Ciaran detested parking. His wife was, he had to admit, far cooler when it came to backing into tight spaces. He imagined Maeve watching him as he reversed and moved forward, reversed and moved forward, tugging furiously at the steering wheel left, then right, then left, then right, like a desperate sea captain trying to right a ship in a battering storm. At last, he turned off the engine, his heart hammering. His face felt coated in sweat. The car was parked so close to the SUV on his side that he could only open his door an inch. He had to clamber over the seats and squeeze out on the passenger side.

He walked down Dame Street head down, hands in his pockets. Like a man pawing the grass for a lost contact lens, he was searching his mind desperately for an idea, a memory, a notion, a headline. What if he never wrote another novel? He hadn't written well in eight months, and it was two years since his last book was finished. Every morning, he thudded down in front of the computer and typed out words, but they were dry and tasteless as old raisins. No juice, he had no juice in him anymore. He had used his childhood, his first marriage, every love affair before Maeve. He had tried to write historical fiction, but he couldn't make it real for himself. He wasn't that kind of writer. What if he had used himself up? He was beginning to panic.

Finding himself staring into the great glass wall of the Hodges Figgis bookstore, he glimpsed his own reflection in the glass:

scant, unkempt hair flying over his head in the breeze, bags under his eyes, his gangly, lumbering body hunched against the cold, hands in the pockets of his shapeless down jacket. Dispirited, he stalked into the bookstore and automatically made his way to the fiction section, scanning the shelves for his own work. They had single copies of three of his novels. He reached down and pulled one of the books out—his first real success. A novella, it seemed shamefully flimsy to him now, the pages flopping over in his thick fingers like a limp wrist. He took the book in both hands, stiffening it, and peered at the author photo. A slender, thirty-year-old man in a tweed jacket looked out at him with a bemused expression: shoulder-length hair, mouth turned up in one corner—there was something questioning and arrogant in his gaze. Ciaran felt no sense of connection to that young writer; what's more, he reckoned if he met him, he wouldn't like him much.

Ciaran knew he was digging himself into a good old fug. Not just a bad mood, but a trench he would be inhabiting for a long time. He felt a sour, familiar comfort as he moled his way into this darkness. There was something almost reassuring about the descent—down, down, down—to a place where no one could reach him, where he loved no one, and no one loved him. There was pleasure—yes, he confessed it, knew it: there was onanistic pleasure in his sadness and he didn't even feel guilty about it. At least it was honest. He'd had enough of impersonating happiness, of his wife's faintly accusatory,

involving masturbation.

121

percussive kisses on his head at breakfast, his daughters' wily attempts to make him laugh, his own brittle resolve to make it to the next book without getting depressed again. He didn't know how many more of these bouts Maeve could take. One day he feared he'd wake up and she'd be gone. A woman like that, a humorous, sensual, hardheaded woman, was a queen who stayed until she left. Eighteen years so far, but she was capable—the most loyal woman on earth, salt of it—was capable, he knew, of leaving. Like a feral cat, tamed for a time, she'd slip away with her kittens. He mustn't take her for granted. And yet he felt himself drifting away from her and everything incandescent in his life, like a man succumbing to a dream at the wheel, eyes fluttering shut, his car careening across the dual carriageway.

He replaced his book on the shelf and walked out onto the street again. So many bodies—why weren't they at work? Who were these people? Tourists, students, suits on lunch breaks, mothers killing time till the next school run. Stories in each of them, infuriatingly locked away from him. He peered into their faces for clues. This was what he needed, he thought: to get out more, be among strangers. He craved new encounters. He had been holed up with his little family for so long, he'd run out of things to say. He couldn't write about his marriage, it would be a violation. His conjugal happiness had tied his writer's hands. He would come into town more, he would write in cafés. Volunteer in a homeless shelter. He needed a pee. The old pub on the corner was as glossy black as liquid tar, with gilt lettering. He hadn't been there in years.

Maybe he would stop for a pint. It was time to break some patterns.

The place was empty, save for one young woman sitting at the bar. Late twenties perhaps, a little pudgy, with black-rimmed eyes and a delicate nose, she reminded Ciaran of a lemur. The many silver bracelets on her wrists made a tinkling sound as she raised the glass to her lips, sampling the Guinness and putting it down again after a swallow. She was probably a tourist, Ciaran mused as he walked toward the gents. Dublin girls came out at night. Maybe she was Eastern European. As he walked back into the bar, he observed her. She had fair skin that glowed against the dark walls of the bar. Her lank hair was brown, cut in a bob, with a hard-edged short fringe. There was something sleek and mysterious about her, even though she was plain. On the street you wouldn't look at her twice, most likely. But here in this dim bar at one o'clock in the afternoon, drinking by herself, she seemed damned interesting. He sat down at the bar, ordered a ham sandwich and a pint, snatched a handful of peanuts from a dish at the bar, then slid the dish over to the young woman.

"I just read you can get hepatitis from that," she said in a flat voice. American. Ciaran winced. He found American English as alluring as a cold fried egg.

"From what?" Ciaran asked, already walking down the street in his mind.

"Communal nuts," she said. He looked at her to check if she knew that was funny. She did.

"Where in the States are you from?" he asked.

"I wish I could master a fake accent," the woman said, flattening her mouth in a little grimace. He glanced at her body; she was all in black—loose sweater, leggings, and ballet shoes. She had big, shapely legs that tapered abruptly to delicate ankles and small feet. She looked at him from the side of her painted eyes and asked, "Are you from Dublin?"

"Yes," he answered.

"Lucky," she said.

"You like it here?" She thought it through for a moment.

"Yeah."

"How long are you here for?" he asked.

"We leave tomorrow," she said. "I'm here with my parents and my brother."

"Did you drive around the countryside?" he asked.

"No, we just stayed in Dublin. It's a sort of rest cure."

"For who?"

"For me," she said.

"Oh," he said. And then, grabbing for it: "What've you got?"

"I'm sort of getting better . . ." she said. There was a long pause. Suddenly, Ciaran needed to find out who this person was.

"Would you like to—take a walk?" he asked. She hesitated.

"Just a few blocks. In broad daylight. To see the city."

"Sure," she said.

He paid for her bill and his own, and they walked out of the dim pub, into the glare.

They walked along a canal, the water shivering, silvery.

"What do you do?" she asked.

"I'm a novelist," he said.

"Wow," she said.

"You?"

"I work in a pet store in Cincinnati," she said, sneering.

He looked over at her again, imagining her with a hamster curled on her chest. Suddenly, he had her placed, he knew her American type; nerdy, angry, compulsively wisecracking, often Goth girls who are inevitably chubby and look perfect behind the counters in pet stores, record stores, clothing stores—any service job suits them. They are intelligent but without self-confidence. All interest fled him.

"My daughter has a turtle," he said. "I bought it in a pet store. I found the place a little depressing, to be honest."

"There are very few people who actually love animals," she said. "Most people turn animals into people, little people they can control, who won't hurt them because they depend on them for food. It's pathetic." Her darkly painted mouth, Ciaran noticed, was defined by two sharp points, a cupid's bow.

"I won't be buying you a pet, in that case," he said. She looked at him sharply, as if he had said something startling.

"No," she whispered, a slow smile creeping across her face.

They walked along the docks and looked out at the big boats.

"Where's your family now?" he asked.

"They're at the National Museum," she said. "They think I'm getting a facial."

"And why aren't you getting a facial?" Ciaran asked.

"I don't believe in them," she said.

He smiled and looked over at her. Her hair was whipping around her full, starkly made-up face. You couldn't say she was pretty, but she had something.

As they walked back, she paused at a narrow, white Georgian house. A sign outside read BED AND BREAKFAST.

"I have a room in there," she said. They both stopped to look at the place. "Do you want to see it?"

"I don't feel up to meeting the whole family," he said.

"Oh, no," she said. "We're all staying at Jurys." He was about to ask what she meant when she hurried up the walk and paused on the bottom step, waiting. He saw her in her totality then: thick, muscular legs in black leggings, little feet, erect posture, big black tent of a sweater masking her body, those blackened eyes. His curiosity coagulated again.

"You want to?" she asked.

The room was furnished with an unmade double bed and a tilted painting of a fox hunt hung curiously close to the ceiling. Maroon drapes were pulled adamantly shut. The girl lit a candle by the bed. It gave off a strong scent of vanilla.

"If your family is staying at Jurys," Ciaran ventured, "why are you . . ."

"I rented this place just for myself. They don't know. I'm sleeping at the hotel with them."

"What do you use this place for?"

"It's my nest," she said, lying down on the bed straight as a pin and looking up at him. He sat on the edge of the bed beside her.

"Why do you need a nest?" he asked.

"I always need my own space," she said, sliding off her bracelets and placing them under her pillow.

"And what," he said, feeling acutely alert, "is it that you are recovering from?"

"I'm addicted to romance," she said. He chuckled.

"Isn't everybody?"

"It's a recognized syndrome," she said seriously, folding her hands on her chest.

"And what are the symptoms of your malady?" he asked, looking down at her.

"If I see a romantic movie," she said, "I can fall in love with the man in it. It's pretty bad. I've been arrested for stalking. I'm not allowed to tell you who it was, though." Ciaran nodded his head in sober agreement. "So I can't go to romantic movies anymore."

"What else?"

"Well, I'm not supposed to do this. Renting a room like this is a real no-no, but—I couldn't help myself."

"You mean to say you rented this room secretly so you could—"

"Meet people," she said.

"And have you?" he asked.

"I met you," she said, removing her bulky sweater and revealing a creamy silk camisole. Her breasts were small and pert, a girl's breasts. She was sitting up now, staring across the bed at him with real frankness. A black widow, he thought, waiting in her web to catch unwitting male flies. He must leave. He was absolutely leaving.

She leaned forward and reached between his legs, her hand not quite touching, as if she were warming her hand over a stove, or casting a spell. He felt helpless, leaden, and faintly sick. She had a box of condoms under the bed.

Her sex was stripped hairless as a child's. Nipples pink as tea roses. Her belly was fleshy, springy. She mewed when he touched her, eyes closed like a new kitten. He felt repelled by his desire for her. He wished he could spread the condom over his head, his whole body, to shield himself from this experience. Yet he was having it, oh, he was having it! Faithful for eighteen years, he was gobbling up a disturbed American pet store clerk at two in the afternoon, and he was doing it fervently, desperately, hungrily. He, Ciaran Fox, and no one else on earth, was doing this!

Afterward, he lay there, staring at the ceiling in blank disbelief.

"Will you come visit me in America?" she asked, her voice higher now than he remembered it. An icy feeling of panic washed over him. He sat up and thrust his hands deep into the bedding, his fingers scrabbling for his briefs.

"No," he said, seizing them at last, "I won't." She was sitting naked on the bed, her firm, plump belly creased at the waist, big legs flung out at odd angles, as if she were the doll of a giant. Her round face was getting blotchy, a film of tears dulling her lemur eyes.

He was hopping on one foot, pulling on his rumpled woolen trousers. "I'm sorry, but—that is unrealistic. If you're going to get better," he said, reaching absurdly for a therapeutic tone, "you need to learn to see things as they are."

"Why did you say that, then?" she asked petulantly.

"Say what?" he said.

"About how you wouldn't be getting me a pet."

"What are you—"

"I said most people turn pets into little people they can control, and *you* said, 'I won't be buying you a pet, in that case.'" She was angry now, and tugged her leggings on forcefully.

"I was joking! I was flirting!"

"I wouldn't have slept with you if you hadn't implied we had a future!"

"That's—" He began to say "crazy," then stopped himself.

"You know how you feel about me," she said, dressed now, and calmer. Her voice had gone soft and assured. "You just can't admit it to yourself." She was smiling slightly, gazing at him with tenderness and—was it pity?

"Oh my God," he said. "I am so sorry."

And then he fled. He ran—truly ran—all the way back to Grafton Street, taking the most convoluted route he could think of, so he could be sure to lose her. A grown man, acclaimed novelist, sprinting through the streets of Dublin like a purse snatcher. When he reached the parking lot, he had to stop and catch his breath, doubled over, the heels of his hands pressed into his eyes, as if to erase the memory of the naked girl. He felt as though he might faint. Fingers trembling, he tried to coax a dirty twenty-euro note into the slot of the pay kiosk, but the bill kept reversing back out at him like a mocking green tongue. Once in his car, he raced down the ramps of the lot, tires squealing, and sped home to Dalkey.

Maeve was in the kitchen making tea when he walked in. He stood in the doorway for a moment to take her in. Her long black hair was threaded through with silver strands; the lines of her body were coltish, athletic. Her little paunch seemed a joyful imperfection, a reminder of three girls whom he adored. The fact of his wife made him euphoric, nearly tearful with relief, as though he had woken from a nightmare to the smell of toast. Hearing him, Maeve turned and checked him warily, as if to gauge his mood, to predict the scene ahead. He wanted to rush straight over to her and take her in his arms; but, afraid that the scent of the girl was on him, he walked over to the couch by the window and smiled at her. He felt so grateful.

"How was the meeting?" she asked.

"What—oh shit!" He had completely forgotten the lunch with the film producer. That was why he had driven to the center of town! "I forgot all about it."

"But you *drove* there to—"

"I—I was thinking," he said. "I just—I was thinking, and I lost all sense of where I was supposed to be."

Maeve shook her head and smiled, the thin skin around her eyes crinkling into a fan of wrinkles. "Thinking about what?" she asked.

"I might have a book in me," he said, realizing it was true. "A character. She came to me today, in town."

"That's wonderful," she said.

RECEIPTS

My mother always said, "There are no atheists on turbulent flights."

This was not her line. It was the first line in Erica Jong's smash hit 1973 novel, *Fear of Flying*. A writer in *The New York Times* said, forty years later, that "what most people remember [about the novel is] the provocative expression Ms. Jong invented to encapsulate Isadora Wing's fantasy, the first word of which is 'zipless,' the second word of which cannot be printed, even today, in this newspaper." I, however, can freely tell you the second word is "fuck." Isadora Wing was searching for the Zipless Fuck. Sex pure and without trappings. I read this by-then yellowing book at the age of twelve in brief installments, sneaking into my mother's chaotic room, thinking I was getting away with something, until she found me and asked, "Are you old enough to read that?" That was typical of her—asking a kid how it should be raised. One thing I particularly remember from before my parents' divorce was, we were at a party at the Hendersons' house on a school night, and my mother was in her cups. Suzanne could get sexy, disheveled, and sorry for herself of an evening. Later in life I came to loathe her drunken self, but when I was little, I just didn't want my funny, cutely incompetent mom to vanish, replaced by this other person. On the night of the party, my bedtime had come and gone hours earlier. I got up off the coats where I had been napping and walked into a roar of laughter in the crowded living room. My father, remembering me, looked over at my mother and called out, "She should be in bed, Suzanne." My mother glared at him for a fat second before countering, "Oh, I'll drive her. You stay and have fun, Chazzy." I was only nine years old, but I knew it was a bad idea for my mother to drive a car at that moment. I remember holding on to my father's waist and looking up at him. I didn't say she was drunk. It was obvious. I just said, "Please don't let Mom drive me." Dad was in the middle of a conversation and waved away my appeal.

It was winter in Kansas City. The moon was bright. I plodded down the Hendersons' shoveled drive behind my mother, who was taking liberties with a beeline. She swung open the driver's door of our car; I slipped onto the frigid backseat, where I figured I had a better chance of surviving a crash.

My mother is ten years younger than Erica Jong. She might seem older than her by now, though. Age is so relative, and to my mother it has not been kind. Her bloated, waxy body lurks like a termite queen in swathes of fabric as she trudges through her cluttered house in upper California, cropped hair dyed a puce reserved in the salons, it seems, for sixty-five-year-old women with a great quantity of turquoise budding on their fingers and sweaty strings of it snaked around their necks, as if to say, "Still we rebel, still we are slovenly, still we do not keep our receipts."

I personally do keep my receipts. I like to know what I have paid and why. On the day I'm remembering, about fifteen years ago, I was in fact on a bumpy flight, the kind of bucking and lurching that makes you feel incredulous that you allowed yourself to get locked into a metal tube connected to absolutely nothing and get hurled through space. The laws of physics are nothing to your basic human need to have earth under your feet at moments like this, and I can see why people start praying. But not me. I hold on to my atheism and wait. That day, it was a quick flight to Fort Lauderdale from Cincinnati, for a medical device conference. I was working for Avista, promoting a new range of asthma inhalers. I had packed in a distracted state. Chad and I had an argument as I did so. I was going to be missing our second anniversary by going to the conference. I could have sent someone junior to me, but frankly I was looking over my shoulder at the time, worried I'd be laid off. The company was downsizing. I wanted to weather the shedding of employees, to seem essential. If I could secure purchases of a significant amount of product at this conference, I was looking at a promotion, and Chad and I were hoping to get married. We didn't want children. I had never wanted children. Children led to everything I disliked: anxiety about money, depletion of free time, inability to enjoy your life. Chad was the youngest of a fecund six, so there was no pressure on him. My stepsister Gaby (my mother remarried a couple times after my dad) had three kids, so Suzanne had checked the grandma box. I was thirty and excited for all this time I had to become a big success and not have kids.

Once the plane stopped bouncing, I ordered a vodka tonic. Not something I would normally do before cocktail hour, but the conference didn't really start until the following morning, and I was still pissed at Chad. He had said something while I packed for the conference that had lodged in my mind. He sat on the bed watching me pack and said, in his slow, sleepy way: "You're lucky you're cute, 'cause a woman as heartless as you could have some bad luck."

Once off the plane, I rolled my small suitcase and carried my sample case down the plastic corridors of the airport with that feeling of lightness I always have when I get somewhere new and smell the fried food and fresh-baked cookies and see the people with their slightly foreign dressing habits, in this case the tanned Floridians in their perma-casual outfits in bright hues like aqua and fuchsia and lots of white. Briefly I thought, What if someone here opens fire, which I sometimes consider when walking through public spaces, and I automatically looked around to see where I would hide. The pretzel stand seemed handy; in a flash I was dodging bullets in my mind behind that stand along with a young mother and her children huddled behind me. After the sound blast of rounds being fired and all the screaming, there was silence, and gingerly we walked out into the decimation. I was holding the children's hands as the young indigent mother clutched the baby. There were bodies everywhere, the floors slick with blood.

My slaughter rescue fantasy evaporated when I saw a sign that said TAXIS. In the cab, I put my head against the cool window glass and watched the palm trees float by, feeling sheepish. I should have been home in Ohio with Chad, not flying to Florida alone on our anniversary to shill asthma inhalers. But, I reminded myself, if I lost my job, we couldn't comfortably get married, which is what I had told him as I packed. Chad made a living, but we wanted a really, really comfortable life. Actually more than comfortable. We wanted to be rich. So that was my excuse. But the true truth is, I wanted the promotion because I wanted to be promoted. Just for the simple fact of wanting to do well, the way I was always an A student and hated A minuses, was disgusted by Bs; they looked like cockroaches to me, crawling over my school report. I wanted to do well and be seen to do well, and I wanted to be thought of as the best at what I did, and my goal was to one day have my own business and never have to worry about being fired because I owned that business. That was what I wanted. So Chad saying "You're lucky you're cute, 'cause a woman as heartless as you could have some bad luck" was exposing my dearest wish and calling it ugly. Calling me ugly, calling me an ambitious, heartless person. Woman. An ambitious, heartless female. That's bad, no matter how you slice it.

The hotel had a huge doorway edged in brass. There were tall palm trees either side of it. The air as I exited the cab was warm and calm, and as I walked into the lobby I was just plain happy. There were already medical sales reps milling around in the lobby. I recognized Tom Sanduli. We were both on the circuit. Tom wore a royal-blue suit that didn't fit right. That was the first thing I noticed. His shoulders were very broad, and the material of the jacket was pulled so tight there was a gap between his neck and his collar. He said, "Hey there," and you could tell he was glad to see me. We tended to flirt with each other a little at these events. More out of boredom and the fact that we were both not ugly, which kind of threw us together. "Hey, Tom," I said.

Once I put away my stuff in my room, I hit the gym. I am a gym rat. Short but strong. I looked in the mirror and assessed my abdominal situation. I was ripped. I held the twenty-five-pound weight so my bicep bulged and checked out my manicure. All in all, I was satisfied.

We all convened for cocktails at the bar. I was still glowing from my workout. I cinched that big order for my product with the buyer from CVS, a bronzed older lady named Donna. She already liked the product, and she liked me, you could tell. She said conspiratorially, "I have an idea: how about I order a thousand units of FlowAir from you now, and then tomorrow I can spend an extra half hour at the pool." We shook on it and I turned around and there was Tom Sanduli with two drinks.

"Thought you might like to celebrate," he said.

"Were you eavesdropping?" I asked, accepting the cosmo and sipping it. A little too sweet for me, but okay.

"I read the body language," he said, looking at me over his drink. "You made the sale, didn't you?"

"I live in hope," I said.

We kept up this skippy dialogue for a while and had another round. I was really happy about the inhalers. I kept noticing the gap between Tom's jacket and his neck. I was imagining what a tailor would have to do to fix that gap. I even said something, I think, about him getting another jacket. He was too big for his jacket. Something. I don't even know what I said. And sort of absentmindedly, like it was a grocery list running in the back of my mind, I imagined him picking me up and setting me on his hips, my legs around his waist, and kissing me. I am a small compact person and Tom is a big person. That was my thought then. But it was more like background noise, it wasn't a whole thought. Then it was time to go to dinner. Everybody fanned out. I said "See you in a few" to Tom and a couple other reps I knew, and we all planned to sit together.

I went to my room and rolled on some more deodorant, spread on another layer of foundation, and shored up the eyeliner. Pumped up the volume a little. The hotel phone rang, startling me. I answered it. It was Tom Sanduli wondering if I

wanted him to pick me up in my room. I said sure, then I put
on lip gloss and brushed out my hair. I thought about texting
Chad something cute. The doorbell rang. I grabbed my purse,
walked over, opened the door, and Tom Sanduli kind of fell
in on me as the door shut behind him. At first I thought he
must have had a heart attack, or maybe been shot. He felt like
a hot sack of flesh. That was only for a split second. Then I
realized he was making out with me. I laughed a little, twist-
ing in his embrace, but his face pressed itself hungrily into
mine, his mouth opening in his big head, revealing warm wet
flesh inside. It occurred to me that he thought it was the two
of us doing this. He thought we were kissing. All that witty
repartee we had earlier had really gone to his head. I tried
pushing him away, but his arms were wooden. I was too embarrassed to actually scream or hit him, because that would be
admitting that he was attacking me, and that of course couldn't
be happening. It was Tom fucking Sanduli. We shuffled across
the room together for what seemed like forever, like dancers
tied together with rope, inching toward the bed. We fell onto
the mattress. He was on top of me, continuing to act like a
man making love to some woman who wasn't actually here.
He was reaching up my skirt. This was it. I made a decision,
one that I have often wondered what if I didn't make. I
grabbed his dick in my hand, got up from under him, unzipped his pants, and blew him. I was aware of his mitts flap-
ping once or twice, swatting at my face half-heartedly, but
overall he succumbed without much of a struggle. Afterward,
I walked to the bathroom to spit into a tissue and he lay there,
defused. "Wow," he said, or something. As if we had collabo-
rated on some special moment. For a good ten minutes, I

laughed with him. I made a special effort to seem happy and at ease. We exchanged a few of our signature quips. Then I looked at my watch and told him he better go to dinner ahead of me; I had to make a phone call.

I called Chad and I was normal, newsy, clipped. He had forgiven me about the anniversary. Across from me was a mirror. There I was. That neat little head, the shiny black hair cut blunt at the collarbone, the deep-set eyes, the quick expressions—laughing, pouting, flirting. Out of nowhere, Chad asked me, "Are you okay?" The tenderness in his voice cut the power on my act. I fell silent; tears sprang to my eyes. My face in the mirror was swollen and slack. I felt myself teetering. Either I start sobbing to Chad, or I get a grip on myself and go downstairs.

I brushed my teeth till my mouth was foaming, put on my highest heels, got in the elevator, and smacked the button for the lobby with the side of my fist. When the elevator doors opened, a blast of merriment from the restaurant hit me; I walked across the lobby into the raucous place and found a long table packed with reps. My seat had been saved next to Tom. I sat down, ordered an appetizer and a Diet Coke. Donna, the buyer from CVS, was seated opposite me, bronzed and observant, her fingers, with their long pearly nails, curled around the stem of her wineglass. I looked at that leathery hand and wondered if Donna had ever been in the same situation as I had just been in, and what she had done if she had.

I didn't talk to Tom or look at him, but after a while I felt his sweltering hand on the small of my back, just idling there. I excused myself then, went up to my room, bolted the door, and took a sleeping pill.

The flight home was smooth as glass, so smooth I kept forgetting I was flying as I picked crumpled receipts out of my wallet, straightened each one out, and put the work stubs into the little ziplock baggie I always carried with me to submit to the company later.

When I got back to my apartment, Chad had let himself in. He had ordered takeout and set out the plates in front of the TV. I changed into my pajamas, snuggled into him, and we watched an episode of something. After the credits came up, Chad looked at me a long time. His cheeks were mottled, as though he had just come in from the snow or been slapped. "Maybe a kid wouldn't be such a bad idea after all," he said. Mute, I put my head on his shoulder.

Months later, we walked into a restaurant in Cincinnati and ran into Tom Sanduli sitting near the bar with some other meaty guy. After the jovial introductions, Chad and I took our seats. I tried to concentrate on what he was saying, but I could feel Sanduli behind me; every now and then he guffawed. I looked up at Chad. He was halfway through his crab cakes, staring at me.

"What are you thinking about?" he asked in a tired voice.

"Just a work thing," I answered. He sighed and shook his head.

Chad left me soon after that over another one of my insensitivities. He moved to Washington State, sells solar panels, has kids. I stayed in Cincinnati and opened my own company. It's been ten years, and I love it. I love the chemical smell of new carpeting in our offices, and the sound of my heels on the marble floors of the lobby. I love coming home at night after dinner with friends, or a date, or a work thing, turning on the lights so they're still a little dim, taking off my shoes and putting my feet on the coffee table. My living room has a wall of glass; I sit on my couch and watch the whole of downtown glittering. Sometimes I look around my apartment and wonder at this perfect place, all of which I paid for.

I've kept the receipts.

THE CHEKHOVIANS

The sunlight was strained through the window sashes, landing in great, trembling, buttery squares that carved up Alex's childhood living room so that her angular body, as she passed through the grand and airy space, was intermittently striped by spindly blue shadows, then blasted by yellow light, then again painted by shadow. This was her first time on the Vineyard since she had gotten engaged, and she was surprised by how unreal it felt, as though she were standing on a set for a play. The enormous, handmade, feather-filled white couches faced each other like albino bison, quiet in the green field of plush carpet. The overstuffed chairs leaned back fatuously; the gleaming grand piano, mute since she and her brothers had given up lessons, sat stranded in the corner. And the flowers! There were always flowers, bushels of roses, their stems bundled and crowded into white vases. Occasional orchids, leaching their heady scent, perched on sills and shelves, their papery white blossoms atop long stems like pretty girls' heads peering around to see who was watching them. She found herself blushing, observing the room through Mac's eyes. He had arrived late the night before, and had seen only the kitchen, devoid of servants, thank God. When he came down for breakfast, though, the cheerful opulence of the Palacio household would be revealed to him.

For the previous three months, Alex had been living with Mac in his bony studio in Berlin, then in a succession of cheap *riads* in Tangier. She had hinted at her parents' wealth: "My dad made a lot of money in the stock market," she had said. "He used to be poor, so he likes to make the most of it." But she hadn't mentioned the tennis courts, the pool, the spa, the screening room. The staff. For the first time, Alex truly reckoned with the fact that the man she was about to marry had no idea who she was. That is, Mac knew her, of course, but he knew her outside the context of her past. Their courtship had been brief, intense, and abroad. This place, this balconied, gray-shingled mansion, jutting its chest out proudly at the sea—this place was inside her.

Alex's father, George, the son of a Mexican gardener, was a brilliant man. He had gone to Harvard Business School on full scholarship and now had his own fund at Goldman Sachs. Nothing to be ashamed of there. Her mother, Polly, had grown up in Boston, her father a banker and fifth-generation Bostonian. She was an alumna of Miss Porter's and Tufts and wore pearls and a little black dress to meet George's parents in their two-family house overflowing with relatives—a story George still enjoyed teasingly recounting, proud as he was of his cultured, Grace Kelly wife.

Alex sat on one of the soft couches, crossing her bare, moisturized legs, and noticed a black smudge of what looked like soot along the creamy edge of a slipcover. She wondered at this soiling. What could it be? Her eyes roved to the fireplace. It was neatly swept. She stood and walked out of the brilliant room, down a cool, dark hallway that emerged into a kitchen bristling with stainless steel appliances. Juan, the chef, was bent over the stove. She spoke to him in Spanish, which her father had insisted all his children learn fluently.

"Juan," said Alex, "do you know where Dorothy is? There's a weird black smudge on the couch in the living room."

Juan looked up, nonplussed. "Watch my onions."

He hurried off to find the housekeeper. Alex shifted the wilted, browning mound with a wooden spoon.

Polly Palacio walked in then, wearing white workout clothes. She was tanned and glowing with sweat.

"You're up!" she said, beaming at her daughter.

Alex noticed that her mother's copper hair, much dyed, now had the look of cotton candy, falling in wisps to her shoulders. Her classic face had taken on a new heaviness in the bottom half, the fat in her cheeks shifting down into a pocket under her chin. Alex casually imagined lancing the pocket, draining the fat, and restoring her mother's beauty.

"I wanted to get up earlier," she said.

"Why?"

"There's so much to do," Alex said vaguely. Her wedding to Mac would take place in three days, and more than two hundred people were coming. She had no idea how it had ballooned to this size. Mac had wanted to elope, but Alex couldn't do that to her mother. She was the only girl in the family, and she knew that Polly had looked forward to her wedding since she was a child. Yet she felt largely left out of the vast preparations, as though she were a guest offering to help when the hostess had it all under control. The truth was, Polly was so organized, all Alex had to do was show up and say, "I do."

"Is Mac still asleep?" asked Polly.

"Yes."

"Well, poor thing, he got here so late. Anyway, I'm happy to have some time alone with you. We can look over the bouquets for the tables; I think we should reconsider the tulips. I forgot that Daddy hates them," Polly said, giggling.

"Who's coming to the barbecue?" Alex asked, turning off the gas and sitting at the kitchen table.

"Oh, scads of people."

"You said it would be tiny."

"Well, fairly tiny. The Smyths, minus the son—"

"The singing son isn't coming?"

"He's in music camp."

"Devastating."

"The Comiskys—you don't know them. He's the builder that's going to do the renovation. He's very funny."

"Why are you inviting people I don't even know . . . ?"

"You know Jack and Breda Bruce, the photographers. They love you. And of course, the Hopkinses. And I had to invite the Levis . . . and oh, the Chekhovians!"

Alex stared at her mother. "The Chekhovians are coming? I thought they'd moved away."

"They rented their house out for the whole of last summer, but I ran into Olivia at the market last week, and they're living here again. She was wearing something out of *Grey Gardens*. A sort of a head scarf and—extraordinary. I heard myself inviting them—"

"Oh God, Mom—"

"I'm so sorry. It just fell out of my mouth. Olivia was thrilled. I always feel weirdly guilty when I see them."

Alex nodded. The Chekhovians were a tragic family.

"I can't remember why the little boy—"

"It was so sudden."

"Horrible."

"Then the husband."

"Didn't he go off with a woman who looked exactly like Olivia?"

"Exactly. I mean it was uncanny. Same age and everything. Very original in that respect. I really should have been in touch."

The Palacio family had been calling their beachfront neighbors to the west "The Chekhovians" for years, ever since Alex's youngest brother, Etan, returned from Hotchkiss one summer, fresh from *Readings in Russian Drama*, and coined the nickname. He said, one slender arm draped over his chair, "Are the Chekhovians coming over tonight?" and Polly said, "Who?" and he said, "The Van Camps." And the whole Palacio family, which was large and theatergoing, paused to think for a moment, then cracked up. They laughed so hard. Because it was true, the Van Camps were like characters from a Chekhov play: Olivia Van Camp, a former actress best known for her portrayal of Chekhov heroines, now a wan beauty in her middle years who'd inherited her family's gorgeous, dilapidated house by the beach; her older brother, Hull, a Princeton grad and a bachelor wastrel who spent his days arguing with their ancient handyman and making proclamations about absolute aesthetics; and her daughter, Lara, who still carried dolls around in adolescence. Oh, and a little son who'd died. And a husband who'd left. The family had an air of exhausted gentility—doomed but terribly romantic. And the Palacios—a practical, humorous bunch—held the Van Camps in high ridicule, yet they were all, in their own way, fascinated by them.

Lara Van Camp lay prone on the shore, head propped on her palm, perpendicular to the ocean, and disregarded the surf as it drew up her like a blanket, foaming her meaty legs, her round hips, then retreated, leaving her flesh glazed and shining. The girl used her free hand to trace circles in the wet sand. She had been reclining for a solid hour in that awkward place, as beachgoers stepped to the left and right of her and children sped into the waves. It was like she was in a trance, her mother thought as she reorganized the beach basket, rolling up towels around tubes of sunscreen. It was a place where one dropped something, or walked through, the exact place where the lovers in *From Here to Eternity* had their famous kiss; not a spot to park oneself and play with mud—not a girl of fourteen who looks eighteen. And that bathing suit was too small. Sighing, Olivia picked her way across the hot sand, to the cool edge of the water, and looked down at her daughter.

"Lara, honey. Are you all right?" she asked with her cigarette voice.

"Mhm."

"Do you want to go for a walk?"

"No, thanks."

"A run? Read?"

"I'm fine."

Olivia was tempted to offer her daughter a snack to lift her blood sugar, but under the circumstances, she thought better of it. There had been quite enough snacking on Lara's part already. What this one needed was activity. Olivia retreated to her chair, shrinking gratefully into the soothing shadow of her umbrella. The child would get sunburned; all her sunscreen was getting washed off by the sea.

At last, Lara rose. She felt the weight of her breasts, still so surprising, and the thickness of her new thighs. A little girl streaked by her, running into the water. Long legs, narrow torso, she looked like Lara eight months before. Lara glanced about swiftly to see if anyone was watching her. There was a man. Floppy hat, loose bathing trunks. He gave her a drilling, inquisitive look. It had all happened in an instant, this body. She hadn't been prepared. She walked heavily over to her mother's umbrella. In the glare, she could see only the long, brown shins and high-arched dancer's feet.

"Sweet girl," purred her mother from the darkness. "Come in the shade."

The girl crouched down and hopped like a huge bunny onto a white bath towel.

"You shouldn't use these towels," Lara said. "These are house towels."

"I had to," said Olivia. "It was either that or no towels at all."

"They'll be dirty," said the child, curling up. "Because of the sand."

"Why not let me worry about that," said Olivia. "You worry about having a good time." The girl released a snort. "What?" said Olivia. "Are you miserable?"

"No," said the girl. "It's just funny to *worry* about having a good time. Because when you're having a good time, you're not supposed to be worried."

"Wrong again," pronounced Olivia.

The girl let her torso twist back onto the towel, her hips still stacked up, and stared at the red cloth of the umbrella above, where light pressed into the weave, wanting in. One of her feet had escaped the purview of its canopy; she felt the hot sun on her skin and wiggled her toes, grinding the wet sand between them. She wondered if God knew she was there, if he saw her at this moment. She imagined lying in the palm of his hand. It made her so peaceful to think that. It felt like a kind of hammock.

Olivia was in the kitchen, slicing cucumbers for lunch. She couldn't think of a cooler thing to do on such a hot day. The windows were open, but there was no breeze; the white, lacy curtains, which had been put up before she was born, hung undisturbed. The large kitchen, with its blue-green walls, the pearly dinette table and matching Naugahyde chairs, the black-and-white linoleum floor, seemed frozen in time. Nothing had been changed, not really, in decades. Olivia's brother, Hull, wandered in. His thin, naked torso was spattered with light green paint. There were flecks of it in his silver chest hair. He wore a blue bandanna tied rakishly to the side of his skinny neck.

"What the hell have you been doing?" asked Olivia.

"Painting your fence with Bukowski," said Hull pointedly. "He found three half-empty cans of Arsenic Green in the shed. We couldn't resist." Jed Bukowski was the seventy-year-old handyman, the last relic of a staff that had been gradually pared away as all the Van Camp money was cooked off. Originating in a nineteenth-century lead mine in Colorado, the story of the Van Camp family had been one of steady downward mobility for about a hundred years.

"Have you been drinking?" asked Olivia.

"Not particularly," said Hull. "That child of yours is splat in the middle of the driveway."

"What do you mean, 'splat'?" said Olivia, with a hint of alarm.

"What's the word? Anyway, she's blocking the way in. She's lying on the driveway, behind a table with a huge cake on it."

"She's trying to sell it, isn't she?" said Olivia. "She made it herself. You ought to buy a piece. Any normal uncle would have done so already."

"I'm going to," said Hull. "I just need a glass of water." He filled a glass from the tap as Olivia walked outside and stood on the splintered porch, surveying the newly green fence. It was a pretty, old-fashioned color. The hunchbacked and tremulous Bukowski was painting the last of the posts with extreme concentration. Olivia took a cigarette from the pack in her shirt pocket and lit up. Lara was lying on the driveway, staring at the sky. An enormous yellow cake melted on a rickety pine table inches from her splayed feet in their cheap blue sneakers, chosen from a barrel of shoes in a store that also sold turkeys and enormous jars of mayonnaise.

"Honey?" called Olivia.

The girl shifted her head.

"Would you care for a glass of cool lemonade?"

Lara turned back to see her slender, elegant mother standing on the broken-down porch cluttered with an old mattress, a broken dryer, and a blue tricycle.

"We should sell lemonade!" the girl bellowed back.

Lara sat up and watched the little spectrums of blue and red and yellow light exploding from the cut-crystal pitcher of lemonade Olivia was carrying toward her. The ice made gentle plinking sounds as her mother walked like a doe, unfolding her lovely, somewhat wasted legs with each step. She wore shredded pink ballet shoes and an old pair of misshapen red shorts—she was beautiful, despite the outfit—and set the radiant pitcher on the feeble table, beside the cake, gently letting go of the silver handle.

"This cake looks so luscious," she said to the girl. "I can't believe you made it."

"I haven't sold one piece."

"Hull said he would love some."

"When he pays me, I'll cut him a slice," the girl said solemnly, lying back down and staring up at the sky. Olivia wondered how her child had learned to drive such a hard bargain when she herself had never managed to ask for one single thing extra in her life.

Acting in the theater had been a deep pleasure for Olivia, and she had been wonderful at it. Her high forehead, delicate jawline, and clear eyes gave her the look of a Nordic Madonna. Her fair hair fell in fine ringlets about her face. She pierced the darkest roles like an enchanted princess entering an evil forest. Even painful parts shielded her from life. When she was in a play, she felt ensconced in the story, protected and fearless. She played Lyubov Andreyevna in *The Cherry Orchard* with tragic abandon, Irina Arkadina in *The Seagull* with manic force, Nora in *A Doll's House* with a frightening, childlike power. Her specialty was nineteenth-century women, but she was also known for more contemporary heroines. She had worked with Albee, and Kushner had reportedly loved her. When she met Ned, though, and had the children, gradually she built a new story around herself—the story of her family, like a house that sheltered her. She needed little else. With no natural ambition, only talent, Olivia drifted away from her acting career. Ned and the children were enough. Now, stripped of a husband, her little boy dead, her daughter increasingly uncommunicative, she found herself exposed and heartbroken. And also, just plain broke. The payments she had been getting from the family trust had dwindled to a trickle. She had called her old acting agent, and he seemed enthusiastic. But, despite having returned to the maiden name she was known for (and, in a rare act of defiance, changing her children's surname to Van Camp, erasing the last traces of the husband who had erased himself), she got no offers. Never a proud person, she had gotten a job in a yarn shop in Edgartown, but she felt so approximate about everything, and people were so exacting. She made mistakes with change, flustered, unable to concentrate on any task, permanently embarrassed. She had lost her confidence, she supposed, and was quietly fired by the genteel Japanese lady who owned the shop. "Don't take off your coat, please," Mrs. Namiki had said softly one morning as Olivia arrived for work. She didn't hold it against the woman. She went into the shop the very next week and randomly bought a skein of orange yarn, even though she didn't knit. Mrs. Namiki blushed and gave her the employee discount.

Hull had already helped himself to a vodka tonic and was sitting on the porch, looking down at the stubborn arrangement of the child, who lay cruciform before the melting cake, waiting for customers. A car approached and Lara raised her head. When the driver didn't stop, she dropped it back down again and stared at the shifting clouds, her palms facing the sky.

"What is going to become of that girl?" Hull mused.

"She's not exactly a juvenile delinquent, she's just trying to sell cake," said Olivia, sitting beside him with a glass of iced tea. "I actually applaud her enterprise. I never knew the value of money until I had spent it all."

"You still don't."

"What do you know about it?"

"How much does this place cost us per month, more or less?"

"I don't know that off the top of my head."

"I rest my case."

Olivia had inherited the beach house; Hull had sold off their New York apartment, spent what he got for it, and now lived with his sister.

"God," she said. "You're insufferable."

They sat peaceably for a few moments, watching the child.

"She never used to be so sullen," said Hull.

"It's all since she got those enormous tits," said Olivia.

"I guess that must have been a shocker," he said, draining his glass.

He got himself off the lawn chair and made his stiff way down the driveway. Olivia watched as he reached for his wallet, took it out slowly, and delicately, precisely removed four singles, standing over the prone girl, who sat up at last, then stood. As she rose, her arms jerked up, and Olivia saw the table lose its square shape, canting sideways, like a woman jutting out her hip, the loose joints yielding, shunting the crystal pitcher of lemonade to the right and causing it to slide downward and crash to the ground. The cake, still stuck to its china plate, rolled down the driveway, lurched left, and wobbled improbably into the road. She watched Lara run after it, hunkered down, hands waving before her, this big person, this impostor. Olivia felt despair flush through her as she scanned the remains of her pitcher, which was stubbornly beautifying the asphalt in sparkling shards.

Lara thudded down the road after the cake. She felt her limbs to be terribly heavy. Her breasts heaved and bounced as she ran. At last, the cake hit a bump and flopped over onto the plate. Other than a few chips of china embedded in its frosting, it was amazingly fine. Lara looked back to the house and saw Hull, his naked old torso constricted as he guffawed, his face red. The girl walked up the road, staring at the cake, holding the chipped plate from the bottom.

"Entirely my fault," he said, wiping tears of laughter from his eyes. "But that thing is going to be fine."

"You still want a slice?" she asked.

"Sure," he said. "I like a little texture with my cake."

Olivia put out ham sandwiches and cucumber salad for lunch, thinking about the crystal pitcher. It had been a wedding present to her parents. Served her right for using it so casually. She was such a vague, careless person—that was why she lost everything. Everything and everyone. She wondered what a new pitcher would cost, and her thoughts wandered to her wealthy neighbors to the east, who must have cabinets full of crystal, but none so nice.

"Oh!" she exclaimed, remembering. "Polly Palacio invited us all over for a barbecue tonight."

"She did?" Hull asked, astonished.

"I ran into her in the grocery store. She seemed so happy to see me, I wondered if she thought I was someone else."

"She knows exactly who you are," he said.

"What do you mean by that?"

"Well, it's obvious. George Palacio's father was our parents' gardener."

"So what?"

"So you think it's an accident that when George hits the big time, he comes back to the Vineyard and buys the house next door to us?"

"I have no idea," said Olivia, waving her hand equivocally. "I just thought it would be nice for Lara. Lara, would you like to go to the Palacios' party?" She looked over at her daughter, who was staring at a random point on the table, slack-jawed. "Lara, honey," Olivia ventured. "Are you okay?"

"Hm? Yes," said the girl. "I was just thinking." The accident with the table outside had been caused by Lara's new body. Her big new butt had smacked against it and knocked it over and broken the pitcher and ruined the cake. She didn't know where she began and ended anymore. She considered how weird it was that people had bodies at all, and how the whole physical, living world was kind of unnecessary.

"What were you thinking about?" asked Hull.

"I was thinking," said Lara, straining to put her ideas and feelings into words, "how most people who've ever existed are either dead or not born yet. That's our normal condition, not having bodies. The living are the exception. And yet, we're all afraid of dying."

Olivia and Hull watched her.

"What I mean is," Lara continued recklessly, her round cheeks flushed from the sun, strands of her thick, white-blond hair glued to her forehead, "if death is the normal state of things, maybe we should stop making such a big deal about it."

"You're right," Olivia said softly, her eyes filling with tears. "I've never thought of it that way before. The living *are* the exception."

Lara observed her mother as two large tears traveled down Olivia's cheeks and she wiped them away with a trembling hand.

"You're so damn profound, Lara," said Hull, reddening, "but sometimes you're also stupid."

Lara stared at her uncle.

"Stop, just, just please stop," said Olivia, her hands over her ears, her face crumpling. A sickening moment crept by, like traffic passing an accident.

"I'm sorry, Mama," said Lara faintly.

Hull stood and dumped the dishes in the sink. "Come help me dry, kid."

Alex sat on the bed beside Mac and scratched his naked back until his eyes fluttered. She had set a mug of hot coffee on the bedside table. He groaned, smelling it.

"Are you ever going to wake up?" she asked him.

"I am up," he said, shifting. "I'm good and up."

"It's three o'clock."

"I had a bad night."

"Really? You looked like you were sleeping."

"No, that was you. I was up at two and couldn't go back to sleep. I went downstairs and drew till six."

She looked at his hands, the charcoal under his nails. "Where downstairs?"

"The living room, I think it was. Very large couches. Would you like to check the CCTV?" he asked as he slowly moved the cup to his lips.

"Very funny," said Alex, irritated about the smudge on the couch.

Mac focused on her then, blinking away the sleep. He took in her tawny skin and strong limbs, her dark, thick, shoulder-length hair.

"Wouldn't you be more comfortable nude?" he asked.

After they had made love, they lay under the large white ceiling fan, watching it churn the air slowly.

"So what's on the agenda today?" Mac asked.

"Nothing really," said Alex. "Tennis if you want, and/or the beach. You missed breakfast. And lunch."

"Beach, please."

"And then my parents are having a barbecue for people who aren't invited to the wedding. And some who are."

"How is it possible your parents know so many people, my love? I only know six—and we're two of them."

Lara's ankle-length peach silk dress, a hand-me-down from her mother, floated around her, caressing her bare legs, her belly, as she wandered through the crowded party. Her braless breasts strained the smocking to such an extent that Olivia had nearly told her not to wear it—but that, she decided, would have been cruel. Instead, she lent the girl a silk shawl to go with it, draping it helpfully over her chest.

At dusk, Lara drifted across the Palacios' lawn, taking in the twinkling fairy lights twisted around wire bowers arching over the patio, the faraway beacons of boats out on the ocean, the detonations, so familiar to her, of waves crashing against the shore.

She had lived her whole life on Martha's Vineyard, apart from a few months with her mother in Paris, after her brother had died, then boarding school in Connecticut. She had come back to the house only a month earlier, for summer, and—she guessed—to finish high school on the island, because they had run out of money. But she wasn't sure. A waiter with a tray of orange drinks stalled beside her. She took a glass, sipped. It was alcohol, she realized: bitter, sweet, strange. She hated it and liked it. She took another longer swallow and felt a kind of static buzzing behind her eyes. A man with white hair walked by, his gaze snagged by her presence. It was a look of recognition she had recently come to expect from men, as though she were famous, or they knew her somehow. His eyes lurched down her body and back to her face as he passed. The buzzing made her not embarrassed by this. She looked back at him, unblinking.

An unwashed-looking guy in round glasses appeared then. He held his body like a question mark, chest receding, hips jutting out. "I'm Mac," he said. His mouth was large, his lips chapped. "The groom."

"Congratulations," said Lara.

"What about you?"

"I'm Lara. A neighbor. I'm here with my mom and my uncle."

"Hello, Lara," said Mac, taking a drink from a passing tray. "Have you been here often?"

"Yes," said Lara. "We used to come to the Palacios' pool parties. Before . . . before."

"So you must know Alex."

"Yes."

"What was she like when she was younger?"

"Ah . . . I always thought she was really cool," said Lara. "I only got to see her when they came in summer, but . . ." An image of a teenage Alex Palacio, in tight jeans and a floaty top, her fascinating upper lip that never closed, her minuscule hips, popped into Lara's mind. She had worshipped Alex back then. Everyone had.

"You're the first person I've spoken to this evening who seems real," said Mac. Lara looked at him, wondering if he was talking about ghosts.

"I'm pretty sure everyone here is real," she said earnestly. Mac laughed.

"I mean, you don't seem fake," he said. "The people I've met so far are polite but not genuine. Except for my girl, of course."

"Oh," said Lara. Mac was watching her with curiosity. Lara glanced to the ground, embarrassed. Often, she misunderstood what people were saying. She was a young fourteen, a little girl, really, hiding in the body of a woman, which created confusion for herself and everyone else.

"Good to meet you, Lara," said Mac, and he walked away. Lara watched him as he lit a cigarette and stood at the edge of the great lawn, gazing out at the sea. Then he disappeared over the lip of land, descending, she knew, to the beach.

Lara finished her disgusting, delicious drink. She put it down and took another from a passing tray. She had never felt she didn't care as much as she didn't care right then. It was a wonderful feeling. She closed her eyes and listened to the waves.

Lara was a water nymph, her mother had always said. A girl who needed the sea. After a week at school in Connecticut, she had called her mother in Paris, weeping hysterically. Olivia overnighted her a plastic object from Hammacher Schlemmer that produced a cycle of remarkably wavelike sounds; Lara kept the machine going in her dorm room day and night.

She heard her mother's voice and opened her eyes. Olivia and Hull were talking to George Palacio behind a screen of milling people. George wore a brocade jacket and dark jeans, exuding confidence. His black hair was slicked wet, his skin shone. Olivia looked up at him, her delicate arm wrapping a frothy, light green shawl around herself protectively. Hull's worn face was pitched like a tent, held up by his worried eyebrows.

"It's been hard," Olivia confessed. "But in some ways, I have been happy to be home again."

"I can only imagine," said George. "You know, I'm glad to

have a chance to talk to you both." Lara took a small step toward them, to listen but not be seen. George continued: "I wanted to express to you that, should you ever have any interest in putting your house up for sale, at any time in the future, please come to me first. I would pay market price, cash, you would save all the brokers' fees. No pressure whatsoever, I simply want you to know."

"What would you need another house for? To flip it?" asked Hull, jutting out his chin. George smiled.

"Nothing like that. I would like to offer it to Alex and Mac, as a wedding present—or a gift at some point. It's Polly's dream that the grandchildren be just down the beach from us." There was a pause. Lara held her breath, waiting.

"Do you happen to know what the market price would be," asked Olivia, "of our house?" Her tone was strange, laced— Lara knew—with the subtlest tincture of irony.

"We would have to get it assessed to know exactly, but at least twelve."

"Twelve million dollars."

"At least. You're right on the sea. A beautiful, rare property."

"We know what we have," said Hull.

"Of course, you may not want to sell. I mention it only in case. I would hate to miss the chance. I know—that is, I can imagine—you might want to start again, somehow . . ."

"It's good to know, George," said Olivia, setting her hand on his thick wrist. "Thank you."

Lara could feel her mother's contempt, undercut by her need. If they sold the house, their money problems would be over. Everything would be over. Lara thought of her room at home, how empty it seemed in the night without Teddy to wander in and snuggle into her daybed. She found herself walking carefully down the steep wooden steps to the beach, holding the rope banister in one hand, her third cocktail in the other. She felt cut loose, lost, like a forgotten astronaut twirling in space.

The sand along the edge of the sea was cool and moist. Lara's feet felt rubbery as she splashed them in the silt. Every few steps, the water stroked her ankles. Her lips were slightly numb. She wondered if she had reached her house yet and looked up at the familiar bluff to see Mac sitting in the sand, facing the waves. He was right there, staring at her. She realized she'd been hoping to find him; a little balloon of happiness rose in her belly. She stopped, holding her diaphanous dress down with one hand as the fine silk billowed around her in the breeze.

"Venus on the half shell," he said.

Lara came and sat next to him, dribbling the cocktail in the sand. "Oops," she said.

"Just as well."

"I've seen that Venus painting. Botticelli, right?"

"In Florence?"

"Yes. After . . . Last year, my mother and I went on a trip to Italy. We saw loads of paintings, and that was one of my favorites."

"You travel often?" Mac asked.

She shook her head. "I grew up here and we never really

left much, that's my house up there, can you see it? It was my grandparents'. We lived there always until my mother moved to Paris and I went to boarding school because, um . . . my little brother died."

"Oh, God."

"He got a tiny cut in school when he was playing sports and then he was throwing up when he came home, and everybody thought it was a stomach bug and my mother put him to bed, but it was septicemia and he died in his sleep. He—he died in my room." Lara had not yet spoken these words to anyone, and they came out of her with the astonishment she still felt.

"Oh, Lara. I am so, so sorry."

It was like vomiting. For the first time since Teddy's death, Lara felt her grief rise up and crash out of her. The hot tears ran down her cheeks and into her mouth; she licked them, tasting the salt, snot flowing from her nose, dripping on the sand. She had a vague sense of turning to liquid and melting into the ocean. The warmth of Mac's arm against her own was the only thing reminding her she had a body.

In the end, spent, she wiped her face on her mother's silk dress and sat, stunned, relieved to have wept at last. She had thought she was broken somehow.

"Everyone is on the brink of death." Lara heard her own gravelly voice like a stranger's. "Living is like walking on the edge of a knife. It's weird how people don't talk about that, they just act normal."

Mac looked at her, the moonlight painting his gaunt face a greenish hue.

"You think like that because of what happened," he said

gently. Lara suddenly felt as though Mac knew her better than anyone on earth.

She lay back in the sand, her hands behind her head, and enjoyed the helpless voyage of Mac's eyes traveling down her body and up again. He looked back at the sea, but it was too late—he had revealed himself. Lara felt primitive pride in the power of her body, yet she'd gotten it wrong this time; that wasn't what attracted him.

"Most people numb themselves from painful things," he said. "From their own pain, and especially from other people's pain. If they didn't, the world would change like that." He snapped his fingers.

"Change how?"

"If people allowed themselves to really feel other people's pain, they wouldn't be able to not help them. You look at these folks," he said, "at this place. All this hoarding of wealth. All this privilege. None of this would be possible without a healthy dose of denial."

"I wouldn't want a world where no one could have a really nice house," said Lara.

"It's a question of degrees," said Mac.

Lara moved her foot so that it touched his ankle.

"So why are you marrying such a rich girl?" she asked.

"I'm marrying the woman, not the parents. But—I suppose maybe that's naïve."

"I don't care what you do," said Lara, looking up at the stars. "I don't care about anything."

Mac shifted beside her, and she saw his head obscure the

sky. His face was suspended above hers for a long moment. In the dark, she could make out only the shape of his head and the glint of his glasses.

His rough lips grazed hers, then she tasted his smoky mouth. This was her first real kiss; she struggled to answer his tongue with hers. Abruptly, he sat up.

"Fuck," he said. "I'm sorry." He stood. "You'd better go up first."

"You go," she said.

"Will you find your way?" he asked.

"I live here."

He paused a moment, his shoulders hunched, hands in his pockets. "You're really all right?"

"Yeah," said Lara. She watched him hurry away, and actually start running, before reaching the stairs to the house, which he took two at a time until he crested the Palacios' lawn, and a little cheer went up to greet him.

Lara stood and was dizzy. Suddenly, she was good and drunk. She swiveled around and spotted her house high up on the bluff. The moon illuminated the slate roof, the weathered shingles. The long grass that furred the dune rippled in the wind. She started for home, weaving.

The climb up the bluff, normally so natural for Lara, felt endless. Her bare feet clawed the crumbling sand as she took each step, her body leaden. She retched, staggered forward, and lay down. Sensing sleep coming on, she forced herself to get up. She had lost her sandals and her mother's shawl. The house was unlocked. She climbed upstairs on all fours, reached her room, and collapsed onto the bed, her eyes open. The room revolved in ghostly transparency. Soon it would evaporate. If Olivia sold the house to the Palacios, she'd move back to Paris, send Lara back to boarding school. The children of Alex and Mac would sleep in this room. Lara wondered if Teddy's spirit could come with her wherever she went, or if he would be stuck here. She would have to live for the two of them now. She wondered why God let such bad things happen in the world. Maybe he couldn't help it. She felt sorry for God then, imagining how sad he must be about Teddy. It must be terrible to be God and yet powerless to save a little boy. She heard her mother's car in the drive, Olivia and Hull's footsteps running up the stairs, their voices calling her name. As her eyes fluttered shut, Lara murmured, "Goodbye, old house," and then, a smile rising to curl the very edges of her mouth, "Hello . . ." Sliding into a dream, she read the words "new life," in green paint, on a gray-shingled wall.

ACKNOWLEDGMENTS

I would like to thank my agent, Sarah Chalfant, and my editor, Jonathan Galassi, for shepherding these stories over many years; my early readers, Barbara Browning and Michael Ray, for the writing advice; and my beloved Daniel, Ronan, Cashel, and Gabriel, for everything.

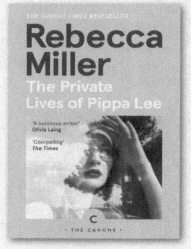

'Miller is a brilliantly observant writer with a sharp eye'
Daily Mail

CANON‖GATE